LuLLaY

Portland ME:
a Christmas Novella

FREYA BARKER

LULLAY

ISBN: 978-1-988733-32-6

Cover Design:
RE&D - Margreet Asselbergs

Editing:
Karen Hrdlicka

Proofing:
Joanne Thompson

DEDICATION

To Mom, who was a parent to many more than just her own children, turning her house into a home for all.

To everyone who, like her, provide the safety of shelter and family to those who have none.

The spirit of Christmas can't be found in the perfect turkey, the finest decorations, or the copious gifts.

The true spirit of Christmas lives in those who open their arms, their homes, their hearts to all.

CHAPTER ONE

Matt

"Be careful on the road."

I look over at Sydney, who showed up with a cooler of food, just as I was loading my bag in the car. Even though Syd is not that much older than I am, she likes to fuss over me like a mother hen. I love her as a big sister, so I let her. She's married to Gunnar, who owns The Skipper, the pub on Holyoke Wharf where I've worked since coming east about eighteen years ago.

Then just nineteen, I'd been in a hurry to leave my restrictive family life behind. Growing up in Esko, Minnesota, under the heavy yoke of the Laestadian Lutheran Church, had not exactly been a barrel of laughs. The only regret I nursed was the little sister I left behind, which is why I didn't hesitate driving clear across ten states with winter weather looming when she called.

I've been back home only once, about twelve years ago. My sister, Leena, had just turned thirteen at the time. The visit had been a disaster, but seeing her again had been a blessing. I tried to stay in touch with Leena fairly regularly since then, but more often than not, our parents made communication difficult. The single telephone in the house was closely guarded by my father. He firmly believed any technical advancements the world had made in the past century was the work of the devil, and it was his responsibility to shield his family from all evil. I'd heard that song and dance my entire life, growing up in that house.

I may have talked to my sister a scant dozen times in the same amount of years. Until she called two weeks ago, finally taking me up on my repeated offers to help her get out of there.

"Don't worry, I plan to arrive in one piece," I reassure her. "And I'll call in when I stop for the night."

She walks up to me and slides her arms around my waist, tilting her head back to look me in the face. "Are you sure you don't want one of us to come along for the drive?"

"I'm positive. Christmas at my parents' place will be tense, to put it mildly—if they let me in at all—and I plan to use the drive to get myself in the right frame of mind to deal with them. They won't let Leena go easily." She buries her face against my chest, and I wrap her in a tight hug, before setting her back gently. "I'd better get on the road."

"Go. Go get your sister and bring her back here. Let her know there's an entire family waiting to welcome her at this end."

"I will."

I press a kiss on Syd's head and slide behind the wheel of the brand new Equinox I bought especially for this trip. I needed a new ride anyway after my transmission blew on the old GMC Jimmy. A new car for a new start seemed appropriate. Not like I couldn't afford it: other than buying a modest two-bedroom house on the south side of town eight years ago, I've been hoarding my money. There's just been me, and I virtually live at The Skipper anyway, where the dress code is jeans and a shirt and I can eat most of my meals free of charge. Aside from my family there, I don't have any financial dependents, no family of my own to worry about.

I lift a hand at Syd, who watches me back out of the driveway and turn onto the road.

-

By the time I get to Albany, a little over five hours later, I'm due for a sanitary break and pull off the road into the first gas station I see. Parking beside the small building housing a variety store, a coffee shop, and hopefully some bathrooms, I pocket my phone and head in. The woeful cries of a child draw my attention, and I look toward the counter where a woman with shoulder-length blonde hair seems to be arguing with the attendant, while trying to bounce the crying little girl on her hip. Poor kid.

Spurred on by the pressing call of nature, I turn my back and head for the bathrooms on the other side. After relieving myself, washing my hands, and splashing some water on my face, I walk out and aim for the coffee shop. I'm hoping to get to Erie, Pennsylvania today, but I'll need to keep infusing caffeine. I already lost about an hour due to traffic around Boston this morning, and have at least another six or so to go before I get to Buffalo, provided it's all smooth sailing, which I know is wishful thinking. It's already after one.

Placing my order for an extra large brew, I notice the warbled sounds of a Christmas carol playing in the background. I glance over at the counter on the other side and confirm the woman and crying toddler are no longer there. Once outside, I zip up the collar of my winter coat against the wind. Shit, it's cold.

Back behind the wheel, I lift the top of Syd's cooler to find something to eat on the road. The thing is packed to the top with muffins, sandwiches, baggies with raw vegetables, and bottles of cold water. I grin; she really is the ultimate mother hen. Grabbing a sandwich, I fold back the wrapper and take a bite, putting it on the console as I start the car. I probably should get some gas while I'm here, even though I still have about a third of a tank left.

I pull up to a pump, behind a red Toyota Highlander with Massachusetts plates. The moment I open my door, I hear the child's crying again. The same blonde woman, still with the little girl on her hip, is one-handedly wrestling to get gas in her tank, swearing up a storm. Without thinking, I walk up to her, unscrew her gas cap and take the hose from her hand, fitting it in her tank.

"Thank you," she mumbles, using her free hand to cup the child's head and press it in her neck.

"Is she okay?" I ask, nodding at the little girl whose little red nose barely peeks from the fuzzy pink hood of her jacket.

"Ear infection."

Tana

Shit, shit, shit.
I was afraid this might happen.
I gently press Flynn's little head against me and out of the biting wind that seems to have picked up, as the tall man easily takes over the task of filling my tank.

"She sleeps as long as I'm moving, but when I stop—she cries," I add to my earlier explanation.

"Do you need a doctor? I'm not from here either, but I can help you find one." I look at him suspiciously. How the hell does he know I'm not from here. He seems to catch on and smiles—great smile. "Massachusetts license plate."

Right. That would be a giveaway.

"She's on antibiotics, they tend to make her a little out of sorts. She's normally a really happy kid." I'm not sure why I feel the need to defend my daughter's behavior to this stranger.

"She's quieting down already," he points out astutely, trying to sneak a peek under the edge of her little hood.

He's right, she is. With all the bouncing up and down, I didn't notice that aside from the occasional hiccup, her crying has stopped.

When Flynn came down with a middle ear infection just three days before we were scheduled to visit my parents, I didn't hesitate to change our plans from flying to driving. A bit of a haul, at least three days, I'm guessing, but I figured it might be a good way to wind down from working like a dog for almost eighteen years building my business. I'd even worked right up to Flynn's birth, and had only allowed myself six weeks off before diving right back into the fray.

I wouldn't even have taken this time if my mom hadn't called me a few weeks ago. On her insistence, Dad had gone to see the doctor, who told him it was time to slow down. His blood pressure had reached alarming heights, despite the medication he's been on for the past ten years. Slowing down is not in my family's vocabulary, so Dad decided to brush it off, but Mom had been really concerned about the upcoming holiday season. The busiest time of year for their bakery, and even at almost seventy, my parents were still running all the day-to-day operations.

Almost four years ago, I was confronted with a now or never situation when I found myself pregnant at forty-one. I'd never taken the time to think about a family, I was too driven creating a successful business. Faced with the reality of a child, I was forced to take a long hard look at my life and came to find I wanted it: the child, the experience of motherhood, a little family of my own. The decision for me was easy, but not so for the man who had fathered her. We had an arrangement of convenience, neither of us in the market for a committed relationship, we simply sought each other out for sex. We never even actually slept together, always waking up alone in bed. There were no messy feelings or expectations, and it worked for us for a few years before I found myself pregnant.

He did not take it well. He especially did not appreciate the fact I would not even discuss an abortion. He insisted he wanted no part of the child's life and was actually insulted when I presented him with the legal paperwork for him to sign off on his parental rights. I didn't get this far in life by being an idiot—of course I wanted his relinquishment documented properly.

"All set." The man's voice drags me from my thoughts.

"Thank you so much. I really appreciate it."

Once again he bends down to peek at my daughter and a little smile plays on his lips when his eyes find mine. "She's sleeping," he whispers, but I barely react: I'm mesmerized by the warm intensity of his brown eyes. "Safe trip."

I still stand there, my baby sleeping in my arms, like some half-witted idiot instead of a successful business owner, as the tall stranger stalks back to his vehicle and unscrews his own gas cap. The moment I see him start turning around, I quickly open the back door and put Flynn in her seat, before getting into my own, never looking back as I pull away from the gas station.

I'd been checking the satellite images these past few days, because of a system that was expected to hit sometime tonight over the Great Lakes. Last thing I want is to get stuck in a snowstorm somewhere, so I mapped out an alternate route to Cleveland, heading south and then through Pennsylvania. I want to try and avoid getting stuck around Buffalo with this impending weather. If I can make it to the hotel in Clarion tonight, I'm a happy camper.

I take a quick look in the rearview mirror to see Flynn still fast asleep in her seat. Fitting my earbuds in my ears, I give my mom a quick call.

"Tana?"

"Hey, Mom."

"Everything all right? Is Flynnie doing okay?"

"She's fussy when I stop, but sleeps like a log as long as I keep moving. I have another six or so hours to get to the hotel I booked in Clarion. I'll give you a call when I get there."

Mom had been worried about me driving all the way, and I'd promised I'd keep her up-to-date on my progress. I had even sent her details on the route I was planning to follow, just in case.

"Drive safe, honey, and if you get tired, please don't push it. I'd rather you get here later than not at all."

"Sure thing, Mom. We'll be fine. Give Dad a kiss?"

"Will do, Montana."

It's almost nine when I finally pull into the parking lot of the Radisson Park Inn. I didn't rush and the worst we encountered was some sleet just past Scranton. Flynn has been awake since we stopped for a quick bite, but has been quietly watching a video I had lined up on my iPad. She hasn't cried since Albany. I'm keeping my fingers crossed the antibiotics are finally settling into her system.

"Are you hungry, sweetie?" I ask her after her bath as she waddles around the hotel room in her pj's.

"Cookie," my one-track minded daughter demands.

"No, no cookie before bed. You know that. How about a few Cheerios?"

Flynn claps her hands together in approval. Nine out of ten times I can distract her with Cheerios and luckily tonight is one of them. I install her in bed with a small bowl of cereal and my iPad while I take a quick shower, leaving the bathroom door open. When I step out, barely five minutes later with a towel wrapped around me, my little blonde pixie is once again fast asleep on the bed, her hand still clutching a fistful of Cheerios. I slip into my nightshirt, turn off the iPad, and pluck the cereal from her fingers, before turning off the lights and slipping under the covers beside her.

The last thought I have before drifting off is of warm brown eyes belonging to a handsome tall man who looked to be at least ten years out of my range.

CHAPTER TWO

Matt

What a clusterfuck.

A four or five-hour drive turned into almost double that when snow started coming down around Utica, slowing traffic down to a crawl. I should've grabbed the first motel I saw, instead I decided to push it until I got bogged down behind a massive accident just outside Rochester. I was stranded on the highway, boxed in by tractor trailers, for close to two hours before they cleared one lane.

I was lucky to find a dingy Motel 6 just outside Buffalo with a vacancy, because everyone and their brother was looking for a place to hunker down. Grateful for Syd's foresight, I hauled her cooler into the room and ate something before I collapsed on the bed.

The intense drive must've tuckered me right out, because my inner seven o'clock alarm failed. Fucking nine-thirty by the time I get back on the road. The skies are still overcast but the snow seems to have stopped falling during the night. Long enough for the plows to clear most of the highway. Driving is still treacherous on the slick roadway, but at least I'm moving.

My initial hope I could make it to Esko in two days may be a little optimistic, especially after listening to the weather forecast. Best to play it safe and aim for Chicago.

My thoughts are interrupted by the ringing of my phone. A quick glance at the display on my dashboard shows The Skipper's number. Shit.

"I'm sorry," I start when I answer, expecting Syd.

"You shit," Gunnar answers instead. "You realize Syd almost had me calling all the hospitals between here and fucking Duluth after we heard about a massive crash on the 90, right?"

"Fuck, man. I'm really sorry," I reiterate, feeling guilty. "I was stuck behind that accident for hours, my phone ran out of juice and by the time I found a place to stop for the night, I crashed and slept like the dead. No pun intended."

"Not funny," Syd answers, clearly having taken the phone from her husband. "You scared me shitless, you punk. I thought for sure something had happened when I couldn't get hold of you."

I'd been in such a rush to get out of my dingy motel room this morning, I didn't even bother to check for missed calls. I just grabbed my phone and the charger and stuffed them in my pocket. Looking at the screen now, I see several missed calls from the pub and from Syd's number. "I know and I really feel bad. It won't happen again."

"I'm just glad you're okay," she sniffles, making me feel even worse.

"I'm fine. The roads are a bit slick, but I promise to be careful. Oh, and by the way, that cooler of food you gave me has been a godsend. It's all I've eaten since leaving Portland yesterday," I add, hoping to distract her.

"Did I pack enough?"

"Honey, if I were stranded for a week, it would be enough."

"Good. Well, now that I know you're not lying on the side of the road somewhere, freezing to death, I should get back to the lunch crowd. I made goulash for today's special, so it's busy."

Minx. She knows her goulash is my favorite. "Now you're just being cruel," I tease.

"Serves you right. I expect a call tonight."

"Cross my heart."

I hang up with a smile on my face. Nothing like some distance to appreciate what you have. I came east a young punk who didn't think he needed a family, but I got one anyway. Not the one I was born into, but the one I chose—or rather—who chose me. I can't wait to introduce my sister to them.

By the time I pass Cleveland, I'm starting to crave something warm to eat and pull off the road when I see a Denny's sign. Bacon and eggs with a pile of hash browns sounds good right now. Not a lot of cars in the parking lot, which makes it easy to spot a red Toyota Highlander parked close to the front door.

I notice the blonde-haired woman from the gas station just to the left of the door, sitting across the table from her mini-me. What are the odds? The woman's striking gray eyes framed by thick lashes and fine laugh lines haunted my restless dreams last night. My guess is she's close to my age, maybe a little older, but not by much. If I'd met her at any other time, I would probably have talked her up. Her adorable little girl only added to her appeal. I love kids. Love my friends' kids, to whom I am a glorified uncle. A title I treasure, since I've known since I was a teenager I'd never be a dad.

"Man!"

The little girl's screech has the woman's head turn in my direction and recognition immediately registers on her expressive face.

"What are the odds?" she says in a rich, strong voice, echoing my earlier thought, but then her eyes cloud over with suspicion.

Ignoring the waitress heading toward me with a menu, I make my way over to the woman's table and hold out my hand.

"Matt Savela. If we're going to be bumping into each other in random places, we should probably introduce ourselves."

With a hesitant smile, she puts her soft hand in mine. "I'm Tana and this is my daughter, Flynn."

"Pretty name for a pretty girl," I flirt with the little tyke, who is sporting a much sunnier disposition today, as I hold out my hand. I chuckle when instead of putting her hand in mine, she grabs hold of my thumb and with much enthusiasm, pumps her little arm up and down.

"Man fix car." More subdued than earlier, her little voice sounds like a chipmunk with a heavy smoking habit. Raspy but with a shot of helium, and that little melodic lilt at the end of the sentence, which makes everything sound like a question.

"Matt—and I helped with the car, yes." My thumb abandoned, she dives back into her toast and jelly, and I turn to her mom. "Do you mind if I join you?" She looks surprised, but since I'm already pulling out a chair beside her daughter, she almost has no choice but to agree with a slight nod. Knowing this may look like more than just a coincidence to her, I slide my phone across the table. "Check my contacts for The Skipper and call the number. Whoever answers will confirm I'm a harmless bartender with no prior record. I'm on my way to pick up my little sister and take her back to Portland with me." I bite down a grin when I see one incredulous eyebrow rise until it almost hits her hairline.

When I turn to give the waitress who has followed me my order, Tana's hand sneaks out and snatches my phone off the table.

"Coffee, three eggs scrambled, bacon and a double serving of hash browns. Rye toast, please." I turn away from the waitress and focus on the woman across the table, who just put my phone to her ear.

"Yes, hi. This is a little awkward…"

Tana

"…But I'm sitting across the table from a man who claims to be a harmless bartender at your establishment."

The booming bark of laughter from the man answering the phone startles me.

"Matt? Damn, Syd, I think you should take this call," I hear the guy call out.

A second later I hear a woman's voice, "Hello?"

"I'm sorry to bother you, but a man who says his name is Matt Savela just sat down beside my daughter, across the table from me, and told me to call you. He says you can vouch for him." I try not to look at the man in question, who seems to be closely following my call.

"He's always been drawn to kids," the woman says, a tender tone to her voice. "I'm Syd, and my husband owns The Skipper. Matt has worked here for much longer than I've known my husband. He's good people, just a little forward. I'll gladly vouch for him, but tell him from me I'm glad he's discovering the benefits of a phone call, and I expect him to check in tonight."

Before I have a chance to thank her, she's already hung up.

"Okay, so you seem to be who you say you are," I start, sliding the phone back to him. "And your boss's wife expects a phone call tonight, but that still doesn't explain how you happen to show up almost five hundred miles from a gas station where we bumped into each other." My instincts are usually good, and this man did not really send up any red flags, but the coincidence is too big to just push aside.

"Like I said, I'm on my way to Minnesota to help my younger sister move closer to me. I'm not sure where you went after leaving Albany, but I took the 90 to Buffalo and got hit by weather and traffic, and this morning's start was a little slower than I'd hoped. The weather being what it is, I decided not to attempt to stick to my two-day time frame, which allowed me to stop for a hot meal. And for the record, I was just as surprised to see you and your little girl here."

"You took the 90? Didn't you check the forecast?"

Don't ask me why that is the first thing out of my mouth, but it leaves him looking at me like I have two heads.

"Man want toast?" Flynn, who is usually pretty reserved with new people, holds out a soggy crust of toast in her jelly-covered hand.

It's my turn to sit slack-jawed as he turns to her with a big smile, takes the bit of toast from her hand, and pops it in his mouth. "Mmmm, yummy. Thank you."

"Yummy," Flynn echoes, giggling when Matt leans back and rubs his belly. Flynn doesn't notice the quick swig of coffee he tosses back to wash the soggy glob down, but I do and it makes me smile.

"I can't believe she did that."

"Yeah, I can't believe I ate that," he deadpans, with a disgusted smirk on his face, which has me bark out a laugh.

The last of my reservations slip away when I observe the easy way he handles my sometimes demanding daughter. She keeps him entertained while he digs into the heaping plate of food the waitress slides in front of him, as I pick at the remnants of my breakfast. It's giving me a chance to surreptitiously observe him.

I'd already established he's tall—I'm guessing around six two—and definitely younger than I am. Not quite as young as I'd initially thought, judging by the sprinkle of gray by his ears and in the slight scruff on his chin today. When he turns to smile at Flynn, I can see the fine lines fanning out from the corner of his eye. He has one of those youthful faces that will likely stay unchanged through the years. So unfair. I'm not that lucky, with frown lines, and grooves around my mouth which seem deeper every time I look at my reflection. My jawline is definitely softening, and I don't even want to get going on what's happening under my original chin. Since I discovered a long hair where it most definitely does not belong, I've avoided getting too close to a mirror.

What a weird situation: my daughter babbling with this stranger, while I observe. To an outsider, we might look like a family out for lunch, when in reality, I have no idea who this man is or why he sat down at my table.

"Why did you sit down here?" I ask him, out of the blue.

His eyes turn to me as he slowly puts down his fork. "Because I suddenly didn't feel like eating alone. I spent a good twelve hours alone in my car yesterday, and the only interaction I had was with you at the gas station Seeing you two sitting here seemed serendipitous. Call it fate—or not—but I'm the last person to argue with good fortune."

I can't help the flash of satisfaction at being likened to good fortune, and I allow myself to bask in the glow of a handsome guy seeking me out. I've not had much of that in recent years, not when I come with a child. Oddly enough, that only seems to be part of the appeal for this man.

"So where are you heading that'll take two or three days to get to?"

"Minnesota. Esko, Minnesota, to be correct." I do my best to hide my shock, but don't succeed all the way. "Don't worry," he adds, taking my face twitch the wrong way. "No one knows it. I don't think we've managed to broach two thousand inhabitants yet. I'm sure you've heard of Duluth, though?" At my silent nod, he continues, "We're maybe fifteen miles west of Duluth. What about you? Where are you headed?"

He takes me by surprise, even though I opened this can of worms myself. I just never thought he'd be going in the same direction. My carefully honed self-preservation has me respond with a lie.

"Minneapolis."

CHAPTER THREE

Matt

Her hesitation doesn't escape me, and I realize how potentially vulnerable she is, traveling alone with her daughter. It's quite possible Minneapolis is not her final destination, but if that's the case, I don't really blame her.

"We should get back on the road," she says, a bit flustered as she gets up and grabs her wallet from her purse.

"Lunch is on me," I state firmly, as she rounds the table and unclips Flynn from her seat. She gives me a sharp look and opens her mouth to protest, but her daughter interrupts.

"Wynnie stay."

"We've got to get on the road, baby. Grandpa and Granny are waiting," Tana coos, trying to hold onto her flailing child.

"No. Wynnie wants man."

"Matt, sweetie. His name is Matt." She turns to me, a struggling daughter under her arm. "I should change her before we go. I hope you have a good trip, Matt, and thank you for lunch."

Flynn has a good set of lungs, which she proves all the way to the bathrooms. My eyes follow the sway of Tana's generous hips until they disappear through the door on the far side. I quickly shovel my last piece of toast in my mouth and head over to the counter to pay. Part of me feels guilty for trying to slip out before them, but it's probably better for Flynn if I silently disappear.

I'm already backing out of my parking spot when I see Tana and the little one step outside. Somehow her silvery eyes find mine through my tinted windshield, and time seems to grind to a halt. I'm not sure what it is about this woman and her little girl, but I can feel it tearing at me when I finally shift my vehicle into drive. With a lift of my chin when I pass her, I leave her standing on the sidewalk, looking after me.

A different time, maybe a different place, I would…with a sharp shake of my head, I find my way back to the interstate. It's not until I'm back on the 90 that I realize she never gave me her full name. I did notice she doesn't wear a wedding ring, and she referred to the little girl as her daughter. Neither of those things necessarily mean anything, but that doesn't stop my mind from spinning fantasies.

-

The skies are mostly clear, especially once I pass Toledo. There hasn't been a trace of snow through Michigan, but when I hit Indiana, dark clouds roll in.

Halfway between Angola and Elkhart the snow starts falling, and by the time I get to South Bend it's coming down in earnest.

Traffic slows to a crawl, and the fact it's rush hour does not help matters. It takes me almost two hours to get from one side of the city to the other. The smart thing to do is probably find a place to spend the night, but with only an hour and a half to reach Chicago, I opt to push through.

Big mistake.

Conditions only get worse, with blizzard-like conditions the closer to Lake Michigan I get. Cars are slipping off the road right and left, and I barely manage to avoid a tractor trailer scissoring and sliding into the ditch right before me. Time to call uncle. I keep my eyes peeled for the next major exit which, according to the GPS on my phone, should be La Porte. I'll find a room there.

I know I'm in trouble another hour and a half later, when the third place in a row tells me they have no vacancies. Apparently, between yesterday and today, some of the roads have become impassable. To top it off, a section on the south side of town has been without power since last night, including the two other hotels in town. All those folks had to be housed as well. It's mayhem. A friendly clerk gives me the number for a Hilton Garden Inn in Chesterton she thinks may have a room or two left.

I head back to my SUV and with the engine on to keep it warm, I call them.

"Hilton Garden Inn, one moment please." Before I have a chance to respond to the much too cheery voice, warbly Christmas music sounds in my ear. Not surprising, with Christmas only a little over a week away, but annoying all the same. I'm just starting to think it might be faster to drive the half hour to the hotel, when someone finally answers.

"Good evening. Hilton Garden Inn, how may I assist you?"

"Good evening. I'm looking for a room?"

"What date and how many in your party, sir?"

"Tonight, actually, just for me. Do you have anything?" The woman makes a hissing sound, and I quickly add, "At this point I'll settle for a broom closet."

"I'm sorry, sir, it looks like all the rooms have been booked."

Exasperated, I run a hand through my hair and take a deep breath so I don't take my frustration out on the messenger. "Any other suggestions? Anything along the highway?"

"Maybe if you can make it to South Bend, there will be more availability."

"I just came from South Bend, I'm heading toward Chicago." Again I hear the regretful hissing and I brace myself for more bad news.

"Sir, they shut down the 90 just west of here, almost all the way to Gary, due to zero visibility. The system has stalled over top of us, and with the addition of the lake effect snow, the plows can't keep up."

"Shit. Look, can I maybe hang out in the lobby? Maybe some of your guests can't make it and a room opens up?" The woman sounds nice enough, and I'm plenty desperate to beg at this point.

"I don't know…we're not really allowed—"

"I get that, but surely you see how this is an unusual situation."

"Well…maybe if you give me your name and number, I can call you as soon as something becomes available."

I rattle off my information which she takes down.

"I appreciate it," I thank her before hanging up and gingerly maneuvering my Equinox out of the packed parking lot and back onto the road.

She may not have agreed to me camping out in the lobby, but I'm gambling she won't be able to kick me back out into the storm once I'm there.

What should be a half hour drive, takes me much longer. I'm so relieved when I turn onto the cutoff for Chesterton, I almost miss the taillights glowing from the deep ditch along the off-ramp. I slow down and gingerly back up, on what I think is the shoulder, until I see the imprint of tracks in the snow crossing the shoulder in front of me. Shifting back to drive, I cautiously turn the wheel toward the slope until the back of the vehicle below becomes visible in the stream of my headlights.

It takes me only a second to register the Massachusetts license plate and another one to recognize the red SUV it's attached to.

Tana

"It's okay, sweetie," I soothe as I wrap Flynn a little tighter on my lap.

I'm so grateful I had the foresight to put my emergency bag on the passenger seat when I left the Denny's. Part of me wasn't surprised to find Matt already gone when I got out of the bathroom, and despite the pang of disappointment, I was glad I didn't have to deal with another temper tantrum from my three-year-old.

Luckily kids have a very short attention span, and by the time I walked out of the bathroom carrying her, she'd already forgotten the reason for her outburst. I'm hoping it'll be true for this ordeal.

When I realized the bad weather was only intensifying, I immediately started calling around for a room without much luck. Then I saw the exit sign with a lodging logo and tried to make the turnoff, but

I guess I was going too fast for the exit ramp, lost control of the car, and slid down the embankment.

The car slid clear to the bottom and stopped at an angle. Thank God it wasn't a hard impact, because the airbags didn't even deploy. I immediately turned around to find Flynn staring at me wide-eyed. I unbuckled, twisted in my seat, and pulled her from her seat and onto my lap. Not a scratch on either of us, but my baby knew something was wrong and started crying softly. I've been keeping us warm with my emergency blanket and she just now is starting to fall asleep.

A light hits my rearview mirror, almost blinding me. Those look like headlights.

I hear a car door and then a voice calling. "Tana! Shit, Tana, are you all right?"

"Man."

My eyes drop down to my daughter who has hers wide open, and instead of the trembling lip I expected, the little wench has a smile on her face. A sharp knock on my window startles me, and I swing around to find a very concerned, but welcome and familiar face.

"Man!"

Flynn almost leaps off my lap when Matt pulls the door open, launching herself at him.

"Whoa, little one." He barely manages to catch her and settle her on his hip, before looking her over and then scanning me up and down. "Are you guys okay?"

"We're fine," I assure him, trying to get out but he stops me.

"Stay there for now. Take the baby and I'll grab her seat."

He ignores protests and plops a disgruntled Flynn on my lap before disappearing from view, only to open the passenger side back door and sticking his head back in.

"What are you doing?"

"Gonna put her seat in the back of my ride. There's no way we'll get anyone out here to get your wheels back on the road, and we've got to get out of this weather," he says firmly, without bothering to look at me, so he doesn't see the disgruntled look on my face.

Five minutes later, he has the seat installed and our travel bags loaded in the back of his SUV. Carrying a happy Flynn on his hip, and pressing a firm hand at my lower back, he helps me clamber up the steep slope to his vehicle. Once we're safely strapped in, he carefully steers us back on the road.

"Where are we going?"

"There's a Hilton just the other side of the highway. I'm on the waiting list. The 90 is closed up ahead, so no one can get through."

"I'm not surprised," I comment. "I could barely see the taillights of the car in front of me."

One moment I'm fine, enjoying the warm air blowing from the vents, and the next my entire body starts shaking and my teeth begin to chatter. Matt puts a concerned hand on my leg. "Are you cold?" All I manage to do is shake my head. He squeezes my knee. "Probably a delayed reaction. Hang in, we're almost there. Let's hope they have room for us, so that little one can get some sleep, and maybe a hot bath would do you good."

It probably would, but the large warm hand he leaves on my leg helps too. I fish my Triple A membership card and my phone from the purse Matt set at my feet, and try to give them a call.

"Long wait times due to the weather," I tell him, after listening to the message.

"We'll try again at the hotel."

"Is your wife okay?" The night clerk asks Matt, throwing a concerned glance in my direction. Matt led me inside, carrying my daughter once again, and installed us on the couch in the lobby before turning to the desk.

"Actually no. She slid down the embankment at the highway exit coming this way. Her car is stuck at the bottom. Luckily I wasn't far behind, but she's shaken up and really tired, and so is the little one. Is there anything you can do for us?"

I'm not about to protest the assumption I'm his wife, or the blatant use of my accident, I just hope it gets us a room. My body suddenly feels like I got hit by a Mack truck. Flynn slides sideways in her seat, her head coming to rest on my leg and her eyes drooping.

"Oh dear. Would you like me to see if I can get someone to tow it over here for you?"

"Well, she did try calling Triple A, but the lines were busy. If you could give it a try, that would be awesome. The vehicle is a red Toyota Highlander, and the license plate is…Honey?" he turns to me with his eyebrows raised. "What's your license plate again?"

"They probably won't be able to do much until the snow lets up, but I'll see if I can get through."

"We appreciate it."

"As for a room: I gave out the last available suite over the phone just before you called earlier, but the guests haven't shown up yet. I guess I could try and call them to see if they're still coming." When she checks her computer screen and picks up the phone, Matt leaves her to it and joins us on the couch.

"She's falling asleep," he observes, looking at my daughter.

"She's had a little too much excitement today."

His kind brown eyes find mine and he throws me a lopsided smile. "She's not the only one. Hope you don't mind me laying it on a little thick."

"Not if it gets us a bed for the night. Oh, by the way," I add, digging through my purse. "Here is my Triple A membership, she'll need the number if she's calling. And for the record, I am tired. Exhausted, in fact, and I'm looking forward to that warm bath." I grin back, trying to make light of the situation.

"Sir?" Almost reluctantly, Matt turns to look at the hotel clerk. "Looks like you're in luck," she says with a smile. "The other guests never made it out of South Bend."

"Awesome." He slaps his hands on his knees before getting up and walking over to the desk.

"If you'll just fill this out?"

A few minutes later he opens the door to the main floor suite we scored. We walk into a small sitting area with a kitchenette just beyond. Across from it is the bathroom, and past that the open door to a bedroom, with two queen-sized beds. Matt walks straight to the closest bed, flips the bedspread back and carefully lays Flynn down on top of the covers. Suddenly I feel a little awkward, sharing a room with this man. Not worried—I trust him, he's been nothing but considerate and helpful—but a bit uncomfortable.

"Why don't you get her tucked in and get a bath going? I'm just going to run out and grab our things from the car."

Without waiting for an answer, he heads out the door, pulling it shut behind him.

CHAPTER FOUR

Matt

I purposely take my time grabbing our things after noticing she was a bit uncomfortable.

Stopping at the front desk, I try to score us something to drink. I sure as hell could use one. I was barely able to breathe when I recognized Tana's car at the bottom of that embankment. The thought of that little girl, or her mother, hurt was enough to have me tear down that slope.

Weighed down with our bags, Syd's cooler, and the two cans of beer I managed to get from the clerk, I head back to the room. When there's no answer to my soft knock, I use my key card to get in.

I can look right through to the bedroom, where Flynn's little sleeping body makes only a small hump in the first bed. The bathroom door is left open a small crack, and I hear the splash of bathwater. It's impossible not to imagine Tana naked in the next room, which makes me a little restless. I drop our bags on the floor, the cooler on the coffee table, and settle down on the couch with a beer.

It takes another ten minutes before Tana emerges from the bathroom, her wet hair hanging down her back and her body wrapped in several towels.

"I need my bag." She shuffles her feet, lingering in the doorway as I point at the bigger one I think is hers. "It's the other one, with the orange zipper."

Grabbing the right one, I walk up to her. I try hard—and fail miserably—not to stare at the trail of water droplets running down her skin and disappearing in the hint of cleavage visible above the tightly clenched towel. Forcing my eyes up to hers, I can't help but notice her teeth sinking in her lush bottom lip when I approach. Handing over the bag—our fingers brush—and I'm surprised to see the rush of heat I feel to be reflected back in her gaze.

I'm not sure what it is about this woman that draws me in. Sure, she's fucking gorgeous with those expressive eyes, lush lips, and enticing curves, but I've been around gorgeous women enough in my life to know that there is something more. There's an air of self-assuredness around her. A sense of confidence that comes from knowing exactly where you stand in life. A depth of maturity I find so often lacking in some of the women I encounter and am clearly attracted to. I'm convinced Tana will have no problems telling me exactly what she does and doesn't like.

Fuck yeah, I'm interested—and so is my less than mature cock.

Mind over matter, I resolutely turn back to my perch on the couch, taking a good swig of my beer to lubricate my suddenly dry throat. Get a grip, her kid is asleep just a few feet away.

"Is that one for me?" she asks, more collected now that she's dressed.

Sort of. The tight yoga pants and fitted shirt leave more to the imagination than those bulky towels did.

"It is, and if you're hungry, there is food in the cooler. Courtesy of Syd."

"Did you call her already?" Tana asks, while digging to find herself something to nosh on. She pulls out a baggie of vegetables and some sliced cheese. "This good for you?"

"Perfect, and no, I forgot. I'll do it right now."

When I slip my phone from my pocket, Tana makes a move to get back up—presumably to give me some privacy—but I quickly reach out and press a hand to her knee just as Syd answers.

"Took you long enough. I thought for sure we'd have to chase you down again." I chuckle at Syd's mock scolding.

"We just found a room. It's mayhem out on the roads."

"We?" Trust her to get stuck on that little word and I roll my eyes heavenward. "No half measures for you. Clearly. The woman I had on the phone earlier?" Syd barely gives me a chance to respond, and her volume has risen such that the woman sitting next to me can hear her side of the conversation just fine, judging by the tensing of her muscles under my hand.

"Yes. We're stuck in a snowstorm and since the roads up ahead are closed, just about every bed in a fifty-mile radius was taken. We lucked out."

"I don't understand—you're traveling together?"

"No, Tana's car is at the bottom of a ditch. I just happened to pass by and spot it."

"Jesus! Are they okay?"

"They're fine, just shaken up. Flynn is already asleep."

"Is that the name of her daughter? It's pretty."

"So is she. Spitting image of her mother." Never mind that she's sitting right next to me. There's nothing I'm saying I don't want her to know. Besides, if she is half as observant as I suspect she is, she already knows how I feel. No way my hard-on will let up with her squirming in her seat.

"You sound smitten." I can hear the smile in her voice.

"Quite possibly," I admit with a sideways glance at Tana. "I'd better go. We're about to attack your food supply which, can I say, is coming in pretty damn handy right now."

"Okay. I'll let you go. Are you still planning to make it all the way there tomorrow?"

"We'll see what the weather does. I'll let you know. Later, Syd."

"Careful, Matt."

"We should," Tana says when I put down my phone.

"Should what?"

"Check the weather." She points at the flatscreen TV across the room.

Grabbing the remote from the sideboard it's sitting on, I settle back beside her, pressing the side of my leg against hers, as I flick through the channels looking for the latest news.

It's not great.

The system currently dumping vast amounts of snow along the southern shores of Lake Michigan seems to have settled in for another day. All traffic seems to have ground to a halt from St. Joseph, Michigan to Evanston, Illinois, just north of Chicago. Road closures everywhere; it looks like we're pretty much stuck where we are.

"Doesn't look very promising," she says beside me.

"Nope. I'm guessing we're not going anywhere for at least another day."

"Shit."

Although I agree with the general sentiment, I can't say I'm particularly heartbroken over the prospect of spending more time in the company of this woman.

Before I'm tempted to show her just how not heartbroken I am, I toss back the last of my beer and get to my feet. "I'm gonna grab a quick shower."

Tana

I'd called Mom earlier, while I was waiting for the tub to fill, but call her again when I see Matt disappear into the bathroom.

"Everything okay?"

"It's fine, Mom. I'm just calling to let you know it looks like we'll be stuck here for another day." I didn't tell my mother I was bunking with a virtual stranger, or that my Toyota is at the bottom of a ditch, getting buried in the snow.

"I figured. Your father has been watching the weather network. He even downloaded a weather app to his phone, but he doesn't know how to work it." In the background, I can hear my dad voice his protest, and I grin. Dad is a stubborn old coot and would rather jump off a cliff than read instructions or ask for help.

"I'll have a look when I get home."

"Please. The man is driving me insane." More mumbling in the background, before Mom asks, "How's my Flynnie doing?"

"Sleeping like a log. It's been an intense couple of days. Her ears seem better, though, she hasn't complained much today at all."

"Those antibiotics must be finally kicking in."

"Probably. Anyway, like I said, I'm not sure when we'll get there, but it won't be tomorrow." Just then I hear the shower shut off and hurry to end the call. "I'm going to hit the sack. I'll keep in touch."

"All right, love. Talk soon."

No sooner do I put down my phone, when the bathroom opens and Matt walks out, unashamed, with only a towel clinging to his narrow hips. It appears the tables have turned.

Long ropes of muscle wrap around his lean length—providing bulk—and the occasional glint of silver in his mat of dark chest hair stands out against his youthful appearance. My mouth waters as I take in as much detail as I'm able to on the short trek to his overnight bag. A quick glance in my direction has the corner of his mouth lift in a faint smirk, but that doesn't stop me from ogling his tight ass when he disappears back into the bathroom.

Jesus, woman—get a grip.

I take a sip of my beer and start flipping through channels, just to have something to distract me from the previous minute or two I seem to have on replay in my head. I've barely settled on some televised interview with Henry Cavill—the man who used to be able to take my mind off anything—when I hear the door open again. I mentally apologize to my former Man of Steel when my head automatically turns to watch Matt walking in.

"Should I see if I can get some more beer?" he asks, gesturing at the can I'm holding in my hand.

It takes me a minute to peruse the flannel pj pants covered in elves and candy canes before I can formulate a response. "In those?" comes out unchecked.

"Why not?" he throws back, smiling. He pulls out the fabric on either side of his legs as he looks down. "They're comfy. An early Christmas present from Emmy, Dexter, and Caden—Syd and Gunnar's kids. Figured you wouldn't be comfortable with me sleeping in the buff like I usually do."

My eyes shoot up from where they'd been glued to the fabric stretching between his hands, nicely framing the very defined outline of an impressive package. I'm stumped for words as his grin makes it clear I am so busted.

"No beer then?" he continues as if nothing happened.

"No thanks," I answer primly, pissed off I let him fluster me like that.

Me: a forty-four-year-old entrepreneur, a capable and independent individual, and for Christ's sake—a mother.

I determinedly focus on a smiling Henry, but that doesn't stop me from feeling the heat from Matt's body as he sits down beside me.

"Think maybe you're ready to give me your last name?" he starts, and I try to stay focused on the Dashing Duke, but he's losing the battle when Matt continues, "I think you know just about everything there is to know about me, but I don't have much more than your and your daughter's first names. Heck, we've already seen each other virtually naked and, may I add, enjoyed the hell out of it."

"Oh for Pete's sake, there's a child in the other room." I suddenly swing around indignantly.

"Okay. Is that supposed to render me blind? Because it doesn't. My vision is quite clear, and I like what I see. What do you think I was doing in the shower?"

"Do you not have any filters?" It's more of an admonishment than a question, but Matt doesn't seem fazed in the least. He just shrugs.

"Not really. I'm a bartender, remember? People expect honesty—I'm like their therapist, or priest. They pay good money to sit at my bar, just to get my unfiltered dose of reality." I can only roll my eyes at that. "Look," he starts, leaning in and tucking a stray hair behind my ear. "I just want a chance to get to know you. All I'm saying is that what I know—and have seen—from you so far, has me intrigued."

"Romer."

"Sorry?"

"My last name is Romer, and for the record, I'm old enough to be your mother."

Apparently, he finds that very amusing, because he's still snickering when he retorts, "Must've been a supremely early bloomer. If anything, you're only a couple of years older."

I try to ignore the goosebumps on my skin as he twirls the ends of my hair between his fingers. As always, the best defense is offense. "Hardly. How old are you anyway?"

"Thirty-seven," he says without even blinking. "Thirty-eight, come January fourteenth. There, now you even know my birthday. I'm an open book."

Admittedly, a seven-year age difference isn't quite as bad as the ten or twelve-year gap I suspected, but it's still substantial. "I'm seven years older."

"Perfect," he claims. I roll my eyes, which he doesn't miss. "I'll show you."

I don't have a chance to argue, or to protest, because one minute he's playing with my hair, and the next, that same hand is hooked around the back of my neck and his mouth is engaging a full-on assault on mine.

Holy Jehoshaphat!

CHAPTER FIVE

Matt

"Where's Man?"

"Shhh. His name is Matt, and he's sleeping, so we have to be quiet."

"Sweeping?"

"Yes, baby. Now hush."

I crack an eyelid, when I hear the click of the bathroom door, and stretch my arms over my head. This couch is anything but comfortable, but I wouldn't have been able to sleep at all if I'd taken the second bed last night.

That kiss.

I didn't exactly plan for that, it was more of a spur-of-the-moment thing. One minute Tana was trying to throw up age difference as a roadblock, and the next I was trying to prove her wrong with my mouth on hers. *Christ.* The silky heat of her tongue curling around mine made it hard to remember where I was. If not for Flynn crying out from the other room—which served as a bucket of cold water—I might not have been able to stop myself from exploring the rest of her body.

When Tana rushed off to see to her daughter and never came back out of the bedroom, I decided to make the couch my bed for the night.

Thought didn't play into it last night, but this morning my mind is churning, and I have to admit; that kiss may not have been the brightest idea. Like me, Tana got swept up in the moment, but she is a parent first. A quick fuck on the couch with a guy she barely knows is not something she'd feel good about after. Especially not with her child sleeping in the next room.

Besides, as much as my body is totally on board with some fast action, it's not what I'm looking for. I've had my share of dark and dirty one-night stands with mostly anonymous women, whose faces all blend together. Not something I'm particularly proud of, but it worked for me at the time.

It hasn't for a while now, though.

I'm not sure what it is I'm looking for with Tana. Fuck, other than her last name, I still don't know much about her. Something I'm hoping we'll have time to change today.

Putting my feet on the floor, I get up and pad over to the window, peeling back the curtain. I can barely see the cars in the parking lot. The snow doesn't look like it's let up at all.

"He's not sweeping!" I swing around at the bright chirp of Flynn's voice as she skips over to me. Tana lingers in the bathroom door.

The little girl wraps herself around my leg and looks up with a wide smile on her face.

"Morning, sunshine." I reach down to pick her up, settle her on my hip, and smile back.

"I's hungry. You have Cheerios?" Looking into that face, full of hopeful expectation, I wish I had a truckload of Cheerios. "Mommy's all gone." She sticks out her bottom lip for emphasis. Fucking adorable.

"It's okay, Flynn," Tana says, pushing away from the doorpost she's been leaning against. "Grandma has a whole box waiting for you. In the meantime, I'll try to round up some toast for you for breakfast, but first, you need a bath."

She plucks the squirming little monkey from my arms, noticeably avoiding any eye contact with me. That won't fly with me. I put my hand on her arm as she starts turning away, and with a finger under her chin, I force her to look me in the eye. "Good morning, Tana," I say as a challenge.

"Morning," she mumbles.

"Not good?"

Her eyes shoot sparks. "Not without a gallon of coffee, it's not."

I grin at her testiness. Tana is clearly not a morning person either. I can imagine ways to fix that, but for now, coffee will have to do.

"Go do your bath thing. I'm on it." I tap Flynn's nose and watch as Tana carries her back into the bathroom. Then I go in search of a shirt and my boots. I have a breakfast to hunt down.

Twenty minutes later, I walk in with a tray piled high with anything I could get my hands on. The hotel's regular continental breakfast was expanded because of the storm. They had an entire buffet set out.

"What'cha got?" I have to watch not to trip over a very excited Flynn, who starts jumping up and down to catch a glimpse at the tray.

"Coffee for your mom," I tell her, setting the tray down on the counter in the kitchenette, since the coffee table is littered with coloring books and crayons.

"I don't like that," she says, wrinkling her nose.

"I figured as much, so I brought you chocolate milk instead."

"Yay!" Flynn's squeal has Tana come walking out of the bedroom, dressed in the same yoga pants from last night. Today she's paired it with an oversized sweatshirt. Don't ask me why her choice of outfit does more for me than a sexy dress on anyone else.

"What do we have here?" She smiles as she spots the thermos of coffee I absconded with from the dining room.

"Chocwate miwk!"

"Yeah, sorry," I quickly apologize when Tana's eyes shoot to me. "Guess I should've asked you first. I just grabbed what looked good. You found the coffee, and there should be stuff to doctor it with, but I also brought toast and scrambled eggs. A few pieces of bacon, some pancakes, and..." I hold up the small carton and straw.

"That looks delicious, thank you. And the chocolate milk is fine. Want me to make you some toast, Peanut?"

"No toast—Cheerios!" I hold back a chuckle when she stomps her little foot. A handful, that one.

"Oops, I almost forgot," I respond quickly, before the full meltdown hits, and fish the mini boxes of cereal from my flannel pajama pockets. "One for now, and one for later."

I watch as a very happy toddler returns to her crayons, a mini box of Cheerios clutched in her little fist. A soft hand lands on my forearm and I turn to find Tana smiling up at me. "That was very sweet of you."

My arm snakes around the small of her back and—with half an eye on her daughter—I tug her flush against my front and wait until her eyes widen as she registers my hard-on against her belly. Then I lean down and put my lips by her ear. "I'm not feeling too sweet right now." I love hearing the small hitch in her breath as she puts her hands up against my chest and, without much conviction, pushes me back.

"Apparently sweet enough to be dangerously tempting," she surprises me by admitting.

Tana

Dammit.

I blame it on the nun-like existence I've lived since getting pregnant with Flynn.

Before, I'd enjoyed a healthy love life without the complexities of a relationship, but my outlook changed once she was in the picture. What apparently hasn't changed is my sex drive.

With his straightforward talk and then that toe-curling kiss, my libido turned out to be alive and very well. Thrown off, it had me hide out like a whimpering coward in the bedroom after. There are so many reasons anything between us would not be a good idea, but with his tongue in my mouth, I couldn't think of a single one. That's what had freaked me out.

I thought I had bolstered my resolve this morning, but coffee and Cheerios blew it right out of the water.

Sipping on my coffee, I sit back on the couch and watch as Matt's dark head and my daughter's blonde one bend over a piece of paper on the table. After eating some breakfast, Flynn asked Matt to draw a cat. After that she asked him to draw a princess, then a dinosaur, a Santa Claus, and a bicycle. They've been at it for a while, enough for me to bliss out with my second cup of coffee. I should probably be doing something useful, like checking emails or tidying up the bedroom, but instead I sit here and watch—a silly smile on my face.

Who knew a guy drawing a duck on a piece of paper with a crayon—very poorly, I might add— could be so sexy?

"There's your duck," he tells Flynn, straightening up.

"Man make dog." I almost spit out my coffee at my daughter's astute observation. It does look more like a dog.

"It's Matt, baby. Remember?" Clearly I'm not concealing my hilarity very well, when Matt's dark eyes squint threateningly in my direction. That's enough to have me burst into a fit of giggles.

"Fine. You try," he challenges me, pushing himself up off the floor. He hands me a piece of paper and a crayon with a glint in his eyes. "Mommy's next, Flynn, I need a quick shower," he directs at my daughter before leaning over me, his hand braced on the back of the couch. With his lips just inches from mine, he sends a shiver right down between my legs, when he rumbles, "One guess why."

Normally I do pretty well with the artistic demands of my daughter, but that is not the case today. My mind won't stop trying to visualize Matt, naked, with water sluicing down his body, taking matters into his own hand. My raccoon looks more like a giant panda, and after my third failed attempt—and the damn shower is still running—I give up. I get Flynn settled on the couch with her headphones and a movie on my iPad, and switch on the TV to catch the latest.

"Why don't we bundle her up and take her outside for a bit of fresh air," Matt suggests when he comes out of the bathroom. "Build a snowman or something?"

Flynn—who pulled off her headphones the moment she saw Matt—slides off the couch and toddles over to where her little boots are standing beside the door. "Come, Mommy."

"Christ, sorry." Matt looks at me apologetically. "I keep forgetting to check with you first before I open my big mouth." I shrug, getting up to get Flynn dressed in some appropriate clothes for the weather outside. It's not a bad idea to get out of the room for a bit. A little cooling off in the snow may be good for all of us.

"Come on, Peanut, you need your snowsuit on."

-

We've made snow angels, built a sorry excuse for a snowman, and now are pulling a fast-tiring Flynn around the abandoned parking lot on a large piece of cardboard Matt fished from the recycling bin around the back of the building.

"Cold, Mommy." I stop and turn. My baby is listing sideways on the make-shift sled, her eyes drooping.

"Here, I'll get her," Matt says, already bending down to pick her up.

Flynn instantly wraps her limbs around him and puts her head on his shoulder. The blind trust she puts in him is as heartwarming as it is concerning. She bonded instantly with this man, and I don't know what will happen when we go our separate ways again.

Following Matt through the lobby and down the hall to our suite, I realize I'm leaving a trail of water: my jeans, boots, and jacket are drenched. I didn't feel it when I was outside, but I feel it now—I'm soaked to the bone. Once inside, I try to peel Flynn's suit and clothes off while Matt is holding her. Not an easy task since everything is wet. Besides that, she's tired, cranky, and desperately trying to cling to Matt's neck, but we manage.

"Couch or bed?" he asks.

"Bed. Time for her nap anyway."

"*No nap...*"

I grin at her sleepy response. She protests every day, but the moment her head hits the pillow she's gone.

"Does she need pj's?"

"I don't think she'll appreciate the effort," I tell him. "She can sleep in her underwear."

I watch as he puts her down and has to pry her little arms from his neck. The little kiss he presses to her forehead about melts me. "Sleep tight, honey," he says softly, but she's already rolled onto her side in her preferred sleep pose. He straightens up and walks to the door. "I'll give you some privacy so you can change into something dry." With a soft click he pulls the door shut, and I quickly strip out of my clothes, pull on my yoga pants and a clean shirt, and scoop up all my wet stuff.

The moment I step out of the bedroom—I freeze. Not four feet away Matt is bent over, digging through his bag, his very naked, very firm ass sticking up in the air.

CHAPTER SIX

Matt

I dig around my travel bag for a dry pair of boxers when I hear a sharp intake of breath behind me.

Shit. I hope like hell it's Tana and not Flynn. I never stopped to think about that and just stripped off my drenched clothes where I stood.

I throw a glance over my shoulder to find Tana softly closing the bedroom door, balancing a pile of clothes in her other arm as she unapologetically ogles my rear. I don't give a rat's ass I'm buck naked, but if she keeps looking at me like that, she'll get an eyeful up close and very fucking personal.

"Tana," I growl in warning, and her eyes shoot up to meet mine, one eyebrow lifted high and a smirk I wasn't expecting tugging at her mouth.

If there was sexual tension before, it's off the charts now. I resist the temptation to turn fully—showing her exactly what she does to me—and instead dive back into my overnight bag. I give up on my boxers and grab the first thing I encounter: my flannel pajamas. They don't do much to hide the state of my dick, but it'll have to do.

"We should probably check to see if they have laundry facilities," she suggests, as she comes over and starts picking my wet shit off the floor. If not for the deep blush staining her neck and cheeks, you'd think she just walked into the room now. "This stuff should go in a dryer."

"I'll take them," I offer, tugging a shirt over my head. "I need to make sure we have the room for at least another night, anyway." I reach to grab the pile from her arms. "We should probably think about lunch too. Are you hungry? I can see if there's anything I can scrounge up. We ate our way through most of Syd's cooler last night."

"I could eat," she says, a little hitch in her breath when my hand inadvertently brushes hers.

"Get the door?" I move past her, but at the last minute lean in and brush her lips with mine. "We could do with a little cool-off, don't you think?"

Without waiting for a response, I walk out the door and head for the lobby.

The clerk on duty is helpful and offers to have our clothes looked after. I'm relieved to find out it won't be a problem for us to stay another night, even two if necessary. Apparently the weather also caused a wave of cancellations. She directs me to the dining room, where staff has set out another simple buffet, something she says they will do for every meal as long as supplies last, and the storm persists.

The hearty stew and freshly baked bread hit the spot, and I was able to score the last bit of macaroni and cheese for Flynn when she wakes up.

"Pretty good," Tana mumbles, before turning to me. "Do you cook?"

"I do. I never learned growing up, but I've picked up a thing or two working at The Skipper."

"But didn't you say that was a pub?"

"Technically, yes, but over the years the focus has grown more toward the food we serve than the drinks we pour. Dino, our chef, is a master in the kitchen and Syd wields a pretty mean spatula herself. In fact, we all take turns in the kitchen. Especially for our Thursday specials. That's become a big draw in recent years." I clean my bowl and sit back, looking at Tana's profile as she finishes off her own. "I would invite you to come check it out some time, but I don't really know where you live."

I watch as she carefully sets her bowl down on the table and turns to me, pulling her legs up on the couch. "We live in Haverhill. It's north of Boston, just on the border with—"

"Maine," I finish for her. "I know it. I see the exit signs when I drive down to Boston. So you're not that far, maybe an hour or so?"

"Probably a bit more, but yeah…not far."

"Worth the drive to catch one of The Skipper's Thursday night specials," I hint, not exactly subtle.

"It's Duluth," she suddenly says out of the blue.

"Sorry?"

"My destination. My parents are in Duluth, it's where I grew up. I lied because…well…" I smile as she struggles to explain and put a hand on her knee.

"You hadn't seen me in the buff yet. I get it," I tease her, putting that gorgeous blush back on her cheeks. "Okay, since we've clearly reached confession time in our relationship, I should—"

"We have a relationship?" she asks mockingly.

"After seeing me naked? I'd certainly say so. I don't drop trou for just anyone, you know." I earn a snicker for my antics, and gently squeeze with the hand I still have covering her knee. "As I was saying, in the spirit of sharing truths, I think you should know that my full name is Matteo Mordechai Savela. I never went farther than Duluth under strict guidance of my parents until I was nineteen years old. I'd never played sports, listened to music, watched TV, seen a movie, or kissed a girl. If my parents had their way, I would've been an ordained Laestadian Lutheran minister by now. Instead, I packed my bag the moment I received my high school diploma and hightailed it out of there so fast I left tracks."

"For real?"

"Absolutely. Needless to say, I spent the first few years away from home gorging on everything that had been forbidden in our household," I admit with a wiggle of my eyebrows.

"Oh, I just bet you did." She grins at me before turning serious. "You are the absolute last person I would suspect having grown up under such circumstances. Most folks, who manage to escape living under those harsh religious restrictions, come away with lasting emotional scars to show for it. You don't seem scarred to me."

Her obvious insight surprises me. Then again, since she confessed growing up in Duluth—which has a respectable LLC congregation—it makes sense she's not a complete stranger to the church's doctrine.

I take her hand in mine and lean in closer when I notice a flash of sadness pass over her face. "Sounds like you know something about it," I prompt gently, and watch as she swallows.

"Not much. There was a girl I grew up with, whose family was heavily involved in the church. They lived down the street from us and would frequent my parents' bakery. She'd talk to me sometimes, told me about all the things she wished she could do but wasn't allowed to. She got pregnant at seventeen and was shunned by her community. Even by her family. She ended up ending her own life and her baby's."

"Beth Oberg. I remember that. My father liked to bring her name up whenever I pushed against his rules, citing what happened to her as a threat. Called it the wrath of a righteous God. Even then I recognized it for the self-serving religious bullshit it was."

"Wow," she says softly, squeezing my hand. "Small world, isn't it?"

Tana

"Now I get why you're driving all this way to pick up your sister."

He lifts his head and for the first time, I see shadows in his eyes.

"I tried once before to take her away, but Leena was only thirteen at the time, and I was young and wild, with little to offer. That's the last time I went back, but she and I managed to find ways to stay in touch. She's ready now. Twenty-five and eager to see what the world has on offer."

"What made her decide now was the time?" I ask carefully.

"Marriage," he bites off between clenched teeth. "My father has someone in mind. A minister at their church. The man is a fucking forty-nine-year-old widower." Matt's voice rises and I quickly put a restricting finger on his lips before he wakes up Flynn. "Shit, sorry," he whispers, casting a quick glance at the closed bedroom door.

"Montana Memphis Romer." I break the brief, but heavy silence, following Matt's minor but completely understandable outburst. "My full name," I explain when he looks at me confused. "My father's dream has always been to go fly-fishing in Montana, and Mom is a big Elvis fan, with a wish to visit Memphis before she dies. I'm my parents' walking, talking bucket list."

His easy chuckle cuts any remaining tension. "I won't say you have me beat, but I'd call it a tie on the unfortunate names our parents bestowed on us." I'm not going to argue that.

We fall silent for a bit and I find myself focusing on the gentle rub of his thumb over the back of my hand. It's a surprisingly intimate sensation, and the sight of his relatively large digit sliding against my pale skin does strange things to my insides. The simple touch is more familiar than our short acquaintance would suggest.

"Tell me, what made you leave Duluth?" Matt suddenly asks brusquely, startling me with the heat in his eyes when I look at him. "Holding on by a thread here, Tana. Have some mercy."

Clearly he feels it too: the electricity almost audibly crackling between us. I glance at his mouth, pressed into a tight line, and I find myself imagining those lips on my skin, licking my own at the thought.

"Montana," he groans. "Not making it easy."

"Right. Like I mentioned, my parents have a bakery, one they took over from my grandparents when they got married."

"Which side?"

Confused I look up. "Which side?" I echo back.

"The grandparents: on your mom or dad's side?"

"Oh, uh, Dad's side. Anyway, I worked in the bakery since I was maybe twelve. After school and on the weekends. Being the only child, the expectation was always I would take over one day, like my parents had done. It wasn't my dream, though. I always wanted to see more of the world, and I could see how locked in my parents were with the bakery. They still are at almost seventy years old. Never got to go fishing in Montana, and never visited Graceland. I didn't want that for myself. I headed to Boston, got a business degree, and for the past eighteen years have been building my own business."

"What kind of business?" Matt asks.

"Best Bites. I started making organic granola that I sold exclusively at farmer's markets, but since then I've expanded with other baked goods." Unable to hold back showing a little pride, I add, "Even though I still have stalls at several markets, my products can be found on the shelves of health food stores in twenty-one states."

"Wow. That is impressive," he responds with an acknowledging nod that makes me feel pretty good.

"Couldn't completely get away from the baker in you, then?"

"I guess." I shrug and return his smile.

"And, uh, not to make a point, but how much of the world have you seen?" he asks, a spark of humor in his eyes.

I chuckle, well aware of the irony. "Not a hell of a lot," I admit. "That will change, though."

"Yeah?"

"Mhmmm. Since I had Flynn, I hired a general manager who slowly took over day-to-day management, freeing me up. Two years ago I wouldn't have been able to take off like this for any extended period of time."

"You plan to stay long?" I can hear the silent question behind the spoken one and decide to be straightforward.

Finding out we not only live in relatively close proximity now, but grew up even closer to each other, opens up possibilities. The distance in age seems to become less and less important as we share more of ourselves. The chemistry we have is something I'd love to explore, and Matt has been pretty obvious in his attraction to me.

"However long it takes to help my parents get through the holidays, and convince my dad to step back from the day-to-day running of the bakery. His health is not good, and he needs to start looking after himself."

"I get it." His words are firm, but he can't quite hide the disappointment at hearing my return is up in the air.

"What's happening here, Matt?"

He lowers his eyes at my question and seems to be studying our now entwined fingers, much as I had before.

"Have you ever felt so at home somewhere, right off the bat, you could easily see yourself stay there?" His voice is almost timid, but when he lifts his face, there's nothing held back. I don't think he really expects me to answer, but I nod all the same. "That's how I feel about you. You feel right."

CHAPTER SEVEN

Matt

Her lips are soft when I touch them with mine.

The little sigh when she opens her mouth to me brushes my skin like a silent invitation. One I gladly accept. The glide of her tongue against mine is a perfect distraction from the weighty words I just dropped. Fucking hell, I've known this woman for all of two days, and I as much as threw my feelings on the table.

I'm an idiot—and incredibly lucky—she seems to be reciprocating my attention with enthusiasm, instead of running for the hills. That's what I would've done in similar situations: a girl starts talking about feelings on the second or third date, and my ass would be out that door so fast.

I blame it on the bubble we find ourselves in: thrown together in a hotel room, waiting out the storm that rages outside, and far removed from our real lives. A rip in time, a chance encounter, a temporary fantasy that probably wouldn't have a chance out there in the real world. The fact I voluntarily opened up about my childhood is indication enough I'm not in my normal frame of mind. I don't talk about my parents at all and rarely even mentioned my sister until recently.

The light scratch of her nails on the skin of my neck draws my focus back to the warm, and apparently willing, woman in my arms. Any and all thought evaporates when she pushes her tits against my chest. Soft curves I rush to explore with my hands, but when I slide one under the waistband at the small of her back and press my fingers in the globe of her ass, she pulls away. Not ready to let go, I tighten my arms around her.

"*Flynn,*" she whispers against my lips.

Then I hear it, a soft "Mommy" coming from the other room, and I immediately let her go.

As Tana scrambles off the couch and goes to check on her daughter, I lean back on the couch and try to get my breathing under control. I brush one hand over my face, while pressing down on the near painful erection tenting my flannel pants with my other. *Jesus,* I need some fresh air.

In the bedroom, I hear the soft mumble of voices, and I get to my feet. "I'm just gonna check on our clothes," I call out, not waiting for an answer before I slip out the door.

Hitting the men's washroom down the hall, I take a piss, and splash cold water on my face before heading for the lobby. The same woman who was there earlier stands behind the desk.

"Any luck with our stuff? Room 109?"

"It should be done in another fifteen minutes or so."

"Great, I'll just wait for it here."

I sit down in the lobby and try to kill time with the local newspaper. It's two days old, but I'm not really reading anyway. My mind is on the feel of Tana's body under my hands.

"Mr. Savela?" I look up to see the woman at the desk wave me over. "Your things are dry," she explains when I walk up.

"That was fast."

"The dryer has been running nonstop since yesterday." She smiles as she hands over the plastic bag.

"Thanks, I appreciate it. Any news on my wife's vehicle? The red Toyota SUV?" I ask, kind of enjoying the way that sounds.

"Yes," she says, flipping through a small stack of papers until she appears to find what she's looking for.

"They called back this morning, but I didn't want to disturb you. From what they tell me, the system is moving slowly east. The snow should stop sometime during the night, at which time they'll dispatch the tow truck and bring the vehicle here. My guess is, you should be good to head out sometime tomorrow morning."

"That's good news. Thanks again."

Walking back to the room—back to Tana—I realize that was a lie. I don't think that's good news at all.

"Man!" The little girl is no more than a blur running toward me when I open the door. I barely manage to drop the clean laundry on the couch when she attaches herself to my legs. "Wanna pway in da snow?" Her little face smiles up at me, and I reach down to swing her up in my arms, just as her mother comes out of the bedroom.

"Don't you go asking Matt when I've already told you no, Peanut."

I grin when Flynn's face drops into an impressive pout. This one's going to be a handful at thirteen. "You heard your momma, little one, but maybe we can play inside? How about we build a fort? You know how to build a fort?" It's the one thing I remember enjoying when I was little. Creating hideaways where I could pretend to be anything and anyone I wanted.

Her blonde hair whips around her face as she shakes her head no.

"I'll teach you. It's easy," I assure her, setting her back on her feet. "But first I have to put away the laundry."

I let my free hand slide down the curve of Tana's hip when I slip by her into the bedroom. Setting the stack of dry clothes on the dresser, I turn around and yank the covers off one of the beds, balling them up in my arms.

"You and my daughter are gonna be making a mess, aren't you?" Tana mutters behind me.

"You bet." I turn my grin at her, enjoying the slightly flustered look on her face when I step into her space. "It'll be fun, but not as much as it would be making a mess of these sheets with you."

Tana

The room is unrecognizable.

Offering to find something to snack on while Matt and Flynn built their fort, I left the room and took the opportunity to check in with Mom, and to give Maggie, my manager, an update on my whereabouts should she need anything from me. That resulted in hitting up the hotel business center, where I used one of their computers to print off a couple of things she wanted me to look at.

Armed with my documents, the snacks I raided from the small store in the lobby, and a bottle of wine I managed to get from the restaurant, I return to the room, determined to get a little work done. Get back in touch with reality so I don't completely lose myself in the fantasy I'm planning to indulge in tonight.

The past couple of days have been a little surreal. Running into Matt three different times, in three different states, in a twenty-four hour time frame was beyond coincidental, making it easy—maybe too easy—to get swept up in the fantasy. Getting hit on by an attentive handsome guy like him, who seems to adore my child as much as she adores him, makes for a dangerous temptation. One that has become more and more difficult to resist.

For the last few years, Flynn has acted as an unwitting gatekeeper, a deterrent for most guys, and an easy excuse when I needed one. However, she doesn't seem to have any impact on Matt to hold back on his pursuit of me, and that only makes him more attractive—and more of a risk. Already I've caught myself trying to fit him into an imaginary future. For Pete's sake, the man is building a fort to keep my daughter entertained. I don't know many who would go out of their way like that to make sure my child was happy, which she is, judging by the giggles from inside when I push open the door.

Furniture is pushed into a large circle and covered with sheets that Matt somehow secured to the ceiling fixture with a belt. The result looks almost like a circus tent. Inside, my daughter has laid out every single pillow on the floor, making it look like a sultan's lair. The makeshift tent is folded open, facing the TV, which is showing a Disney movie. My daughter is cuddled up inside next to Matt, who is leaning back on an elbow, a grin on his face.

"I come bearing gifts," I announce, forcibly ignoring the shiver that runs down my back at Matt's playful wink.

"Mommy, come sit!" Flynn, whose every word comes out at a higher than necessary volume, pats the pile of pillows on the other side of her.

"Mommy has to read through a few papers, but I'll be quick and then I'll come sit with you. I've got some Cheetos and some candy for you though." I toss the little bags at Matt, who catches them deftly in his free hand."

"Cheetos!"

I know I'm gonna regret this. I make sure my daughter eats well—healthy—but the past few days have blown that completely out of the water. Cheetos are her favorite treat, but she only gets them once in a blue moon. I shudder thinking about all the additives they put in that stuff.

"And what's that for?" Matt points at the bottle of wine in my hand, and I can feel that damn blush crawling up my neck.

"For us. For later." My voice suddenly a bit hoarse, hearing the promise in my own words.

His eyes, playful before, suddenly spark a heat I can feel across the room. "I like that plan," he rumbles, as I slip around their fort to get to the bedroom.

Oh yeah, I'm well aware of what I was offering, and clearly so is he. Closing the door firmly, I sit down at the small desk, trying—and eventually succeeding—to focus on the stack of papers. The contract is from a large grocery store chain, looking to carry my products on their shelves. From specialty stores to mainstream grocery stores is a major move—one that could do big things for my little company. A game changer.

I'm surprised to find it dark outside when the door opens and Matt sticks his head in. "She's asleep. Has been for the past twenty minutes."

"Really? What time is it?" I swing around to look at the alarm clock on the nightstand. "Eight-thirty? Jesus, I'm so sorry," I mutter, scrambling out of my chair. "I haven't even fed her."

"Trust me, she's not starving. By the time the second movie was done, she'd scarfed her way through her snacks."

"I'm so sorry," I apologize, getting to my feet. "I didn't mean to—"

"Stop. You get your work done?" he asks, after cutting me off.

"I did."

"Perfect," he says, walking right up to me, stroking his hands from my shoulders down my arms. He grasps my wrists loosely and pulls them around to his back, where I grab onto his shirt. "That means we just entered the adult entertainment part of the night."

I look up into his dark brown eyes that seem to rake over my face until they settle on my lips. I forget to breathe when he lowers his head and brushes his mouth over mine, but just as quickly he pulls away. "Hold that thought," he mumbles, nudging the tip of my nose with his. "I'm going to put Flynn in here, and see if I can order some food. Then we're going to see if there's a decent movie on, settle into my awesome fort, and crack that bottle of wine."

Twenty minutes later, my Peanut is tucked into bed in the other room, and Matt walks in carrying a plate with a stack of grilled cheese sandwiches.

"This was the fastest thing I could get," he apologizes, shrugging his shoulders. "Far from the gourmet meal I would've loved to feed you on our first official date."

"Date?"

"Of course. What did you think this was?"

I figure my pleased smile is response enough, as I take the plate from him and duck into his fort. He follows a few minutes later carrying two glasses of wine and settles in beside me. We eat while Matt flips through the channels, looking for a suitable movie. By the time we're done, he's finally settled on an all music channel, the volume turned down to an easy listening level.

"Give me your glass," he says after I take a sip of my wine. I hand it over and he sets it along with his, beside the TV.

Sitting on his knees, he turns to face me and I take in a sharp breath at the predatory gleam in his eyes. "You're sure?" He doesn't have to clarify, I know exactly what he's asking.

"Positive," is my firm answer.

"Lie back, Montana," he orders, his voice low and raspy. Normally not one for taking orders, I'm so primed, I willingly do as he says, enjoying the slow roam of his gaze from the top of my head to the tips of my toes. Goosebumps rise over my skin and my nipples harden in tight buds. "That body of yours has been teasing me since the first time I laid eyes on it. I'm aiming to do wicked things to it tonight."

CHAPTER EIGHT

Matt

Christ, she's beautiful.

A blush darkening from her cleavage to her face, her lips slightly parted, and her nostrils flared on every intake of breath.

If I wasn't sure before she was ready for me, I sure as fuck am sure now. Tana is as turned on as I am.

Dropping down to hands and knees, I slowly crawl to her, hovering with my body over hers, and even now I can smell the heady scent of her arousal. Magnificent.

This time, when I lower my mouth to hers, there is nothing tentative or restrained about my intent. I mean to feast on her. The soft groan when I slide my tongue between her lips is matched with my own, when she tangles her fingers in my hair. There is nothing sexier than a woman who knows what she likes and how she likes it. Tana may not use words, but her body speaks loud and clear when I lower my hips between legs, she opens in invitation.

Our clothes are a barrier, but I don't want to rush this. Who knows what will happen tomorrow, but there's no doubt what is happening here tonight, and I'm gonna make it last as long as I possibly can.

While our tongues explore, she slides a hand along my spine, down to my ass, where she grabs a handful, pulling me closer. I swivel my hips and rub my rock-hard cock against her core. She tilts her hips and I groan, feeling her damp heat through the layers of fabric.

Pulling my mouth from hers, I drop my face into her neck, inhaling her unique scent and burning it into my memory.

"I was going to take my time, but those plans have changed," I whisper into her hair, my hands already pulling up her top. "Lift your arms." Raising higher, I sit her up and strip the shirt all the way off. No bra to hold them, her tits are the first thing my eyes are drawn to. My hands follow right behind, lifting their weight in my palms. "Beautiful," I mumble, dropping my head to take first one, and then the second nipple deep into my mouth, eliciting a moan from her lips.

"Lie back, sweetheart. Let me look at you."

Her lips still red and swollen from our kiss, her blonde tresses fanned around her flushed face as she settles back in the pillows, she looks like a fucking fantasy come true.

Already she's wiggling to get her yoga pants down her ass, and I'm struck once again by the quiet confidence she exudes. There's no self-conscious hesitation as she slips out of her clothes, exposing her soft belly lined with stretch marks, or the dimpled flesh of her thighs. Her eyes never waver from mine as she kicks the offensive piece of clothing to the side, cocks her knees and lets them fall open, her hand slipping down to lazily stroke through the pale curls between her legs.

It takes me a second to whip off my shirt, and push down the ridiculous flannel pants, my cock bouncing eagerly when released. I'm not an athlete. I don't have a particularly buff body and am probably average in the girth department, but the way Tana's eyes take me in; I feel like that Henry Cavill guy she was ogling on TV, complete with monster cock.

I'm good with that.

Any and all coherent thought evaporates when her nimble fingers slip down and spread her pussy lips, her arousal glistening between. Dipping her middle finger inside, she tracks the wetness to her clit, rubbing it gently. That's when any semblance of control disappears, and I drop down between her legs, following the damp trail her finger left behind.

"*Matt,*" she sighs, when I push her legs high and wide and latch on to that little bundle of nerves.

Immediately the muscles in her legs start trembling, as she writhes under my hands. Selfishly, I release her clit. I want to be inside her when she comes. Reaching over, I pull a condom free from the pocket of my pajamas and cover myself quickly.

Spreading my knees wide, I guide my cock to her entrance, and find her eyes again before I slide inside, stopping only when my balls hit her ass.

Fucking perfect.

"Lift my legs against your shoulders," she urges. With her legs folded up, she presses her knees together and my eyes about roll back in my head. I can feel her tightening around me. "Now fuck me, Matt."

I don't have to be told twice, and with her fingers digging into my ass, I feel myself barreling toward release as I hammer into her. Just as I feel her walls close in on me, I let go of the hot flow of cum, surging up from my balls, pulled tight against my body.

I swear I'm blind as I fall on her, both our bodies sweaty and twitching with aftershocks.

Tana

I'm not sure what round we're on when Flynn calls from the other room, but I know it has to be past midnight.

Apparently, Matt is no one-trick pony. There's something to say for youth: his capacity for recovery is astounding. I'm not a virgin by any stretch of the imagination, and I can honestly say that kind of stamina is unique.

And boy, can he deliver; in more ways than one. I feel more worshipped, as well as sated, than I ever have.

The man is a rock in a crisis, Prince Charming to my daughter, and a powerhouse in bed. Matt Savela spells trouble in capital letters. Good thing tomorrow is the expiration date on this fairy tale, or else Flynn won't be the only one heartbroken when we go our own ways.

"I'll go check," Matt says, pulling up his pants.

I'm still scrambling to find my own clothes when I hear the low rumble of his voice and the much higher pitch of my little girl's from the bedroom. I'm just pulling my shirt over my head when he walks out, Flynn on his arm.

"This little princess needs to pee." Matt presses a soft kiss to her hair, melting my heart. "You should probably take her," he whispers over her head, outright killing me with his thoughtful care.

Ignoring Flynn's mumbled objections, he hands her to me before making himself scarce, and I rush her into the bathroom.

"Want Man, Mommy," she complains sleepily, rubbing her eyes while I help her take care of business.

"Tomorrow, Peanut. We need to do a bit more sleeping first. Come on…" I set her to her feet and pull up her bottoms, scooping her up in my arms. "I'll tuck you in."

"I want Man!" she whines louder when I open the bathroom door.

Matt is already waiting on the other side, and I shoot him an apologetic grin and shake my head. "I'm sorry, she's a bit of a handful. To think I once wanted a big family—"

"I'll take her, if that's okay?" he asks, interrupting me with a strange melancholy smile on his face.

"Sure." I don't object when she reaches for him, wrapping her little arms around his neck, clinging on like a monkey.

Tomorrow is going to suck all around.

Matt disappears with her into the bedroom, and I turn in the opposite direction, in search of my glass of wine. I need a drink.

I notice he did some rearranging while I was in the bathroom. The tent has come down, and he has placed all the couch pillows on the floor, covering them with one of the sheets. He turned it into a large bed and it's obvious he's intending to sleep here with me tonight. There's nothing I'd enjoy more than to cuddle up in his arms all night, but I'm already teetering on a slippery slope. Self-preservation has me pick up a pillow, and head back to the bedroom.

I ease the door open and am struck by the sight of Matt, sitting on the edge of the mattress, watching my daughter's angelic face, his hand stroking her hair.

He appears to have fallen for her just as hard as she has for him.

"Lully, lullay, thou little tiny child,
Bye bye, lully, lullay."

The sound of his deep voice, softly singing my baby to sleep with a Christmas carol has a lump form in my throat. The beautiful song has always moved me, but hearing him sing those words to her gives them an even deeper meaning.

Resolved, and with the pillow still stuck under my arm, I turn and pad back to the make-shift bed on the floor.

It's already too late for self-preservation.

A few minutes later, he walks out and gently pulls the door shut behind him. I'm already in bed and flip the covers down on his side. He recognizes the invitation and wordlessly slips between the sheets, pulling me straight into his arms, tucking my head under his chin where I snuggle in.

We lie like that for a while, just softly stroking and breathing each other in. Memorizing touch and scent.

"I wish—" he starts, but I stop him with my fingers to his lips.

"*Hush,*" I whisper. I don't want to hear anything that might spoil tonight's bittersweet magic. If wishes were horses, beggars would ride. "Just hold me."

Matt

There is no point in trying to resist either mother or daughter—they already own me.

Flynn's little girl voice was irresistible, asking me to sing her to sleep. The "Coventry Carol" immediately came to mind and it didn't take long for her eyes to flutter closed. Little did she know I felt every word I sang to her tear at my soul.

For a while, I just lie beside Tana, thinking about our unusual situation. The fact she'd be in Duluth for an undetermined time, and I should be back in Boston with Leena before long, isn't exactly conducive to any kind of relationship. The different possibilities and solutions churn in my mind. I was just about to voice my spinning thoughts, when she stopped me in my tracks. As if she'd known what I'd been planning to say and didn't want me going there.

Instead of talking anything through, I ended up holding her until we finally both fell asleep.

This morning we were woken up by a very energetic Flynn, who somehow had climbed down from the tall hotel bed and managed to open the door. Her little body snuggled between us on the floor and her mouth going a mile a minute, half of it I didn't understand. Tana looked at me over her daughter's head, regret clear on her face.

As predicted, the snow had stopped last night, and we could already hear the snowplows clearing the parking lot outside. Leaning over Flynn, I kissed Tana lightly on her lips, pressed one on Flynn's forehead as well, and headed for the bathroom, knowing I'd just said goodbye.

Tana already had the room back in order when I walked out of the bathroom. Once again stark and functional, there was nothing left to show the beautiful ripple in time we shared.

Listening to Flynn's chatter from the bedroom, I quickly pull on my clothes, stuff the rest of my belongings in my bag, and head to check the front desk for news on the Toyota.

"They were here first thing this morning, sir," a clerk I hadn't seen before tells me. "The vehicle is parked out front." He hands me the keys Tana had left with them.

"What about the roads? Any closures still in effect that you know of?"

"The 90 was open as of five this morning. I just drove it to get here myself." The man smiles like he's just given me good news. He has no fucking idea.

With a nod of thanks, I wander into the small dining room, grab a few things for breakfast from the buffet, and head back to the room.

"Wasn't sure where you'd gone," Tana comments, a little breathless as she rubs her hair dry from her shower. There's no sign of Flynn, but I hear the splash of water coming from the bathroom.

"Your Toyota is out front." All movement freezes as she blinks a few times at my brusque words. "I'm just gonna make sure it's in good driving order, while you guys eat breakfast and get ready. I'll be back to help you load up," I suggest, trying hard not to look directly at her.

One look at me and she'd probably see right through the resolute tone of my words, to the uncertain hurt in my eyes. I barely hear her, "Okay," as I leave the tray on the coffee table, snag my duffel, and walk back out.

Twenty minutes later I return, both my car and hers now parked side by side in the parking lot, engines running to get them warmed up. Flynn's car seat is installed in the Toyota again.

"Man!" her little voice greets me when I walk in the door.

"We're ready," Tana announces, just as the little one clamps onto my leg. Unable to resist her, I bend down and swing her up in my arms, burying my nose in her still damp hair. "*Matt,*" Tana whispers when I lift my eyes to her, unable to hide the loss I'm already feeling.

Resolutely swinging Flynn on my hip, I grab their bags in my other hand. "I'll help you load up."

Flynn launched a few protests when I strapped her in her seat, but when her mother lined up *Bambi* on the tablet hanging off the back of the front seat, she settled right down.

With the little one already lost to her movie, I turn to Tana. "Hand me your phone."

She looks at me puzzled for only a moment before digging through her purse. "Why?" she asks, handing it over.

"In case something happens?" I throw out, as I enter my number into her contacts and give the phone back.

"Oh, okay." Her disappointment is obvious and suddenly I can't bear to send her off with a lie.

"*Fuck*. The truth is I'm not ready to let go yet. I can't," I confess, and she nods, tears welling in her eyes.

"I know. Me too." Suddenly her arms are around me and we hold onto each other.

I shove my face in the crook of her neck and the right words fail me. "I've had…It's been…If only…" I stumble, unable to string a coherent thought together. "Call me if you need me. For anything. I'm…I'll be there."

"I know," she mumbles.

"I wish…"

"Me too. I wish that too."

One moment she is in my arms, and the next she's behind the wheel, backing out of her parking space. I can see Flynn in the back seat, oblivious to the emotional turmoil surrounding her.

As I watch them drive off, I feel as if I've just sent off my one chance at the life I never thought I'd have.

CHAPTER NINE

Tana

"There are my girls!"

Mom must've been looking out the window, because she's heading toward the car, bundled in her winter coat, before I even have the car door open.

Nothing feels better than being wrapped in welcoming arms when you've just spent close to thirteen hours on the road, with a three-year-old full of beans, and a sharp ache in your chest. I have to battle back the tears—fatigue—mostly.

"You should've stopped," Mom says, putting a cool hand to my cheek as she scans my face. "No person in their sane mind would have tackled that in one run. Not with a baby in the car."

"I just wanted to get here. It's been a long few days."

"I bet," she says, with one last scrutinizing look at me. "Now where's my Flynnie?"

"Shhh," I caution her. "She's been asleep since just past Eau Claire. I'd just as soon drop her straight to bed if we can manage."

"I'll take her. I have her in your old room, and you're on the other side of the bathroom, in the guest room."

"We could've shared a room, Mom," I remind her, but she waves me off.

"This way you don't have to disturb each other. I bet it's been ages since you were able to sleep in."

Three years to be exact.

I watch as Mom unclips Flynn's harness and lifts her deftly out of her seat without waking her.

"Grab just what you need for tonight," she instructs me as she passes. "We'll get the rest tomorrow morning."

The house smells familiar—like home—when I walk in the door. I drop my bags and barely shrug out of my coat when I'm wrapped in an equally familiar hug.

"Princess," my father's deep voice rumbles over my head, as I wrap my arms around his expanding waist.

"Hey, Dad."

"Too long, my girl."

"I know. It's good to be here." I try to step back so I can look at him, but he holds me tight, giving me an extra squeeze before finally letting go. "How are you doing?" I ask, taking a visual inventory of my ailing father.

"Can't complain," he states, shrugging off the attention he's not comfortable with. "Better now that you're here. I see my granddaughter is growing like a weed." I recognize the distraction tactic and decide to let him get away with it. For now.

"She is," I confirm, smiling at him. "And smart as a whip. She talks up a storm these days."

"Bet she's a firecracker, just like her mom was."

"Why are you all standing in the hallway?" Mom says as she comes down the stairs. "Come inside, sweetie. Let me get you something to eat."

I let her guide me into the kitchen, where she has me sit down while she pulls out more food than I could possibly eat in a week. All my favorites. My parents join me at the kitchen table and ask me a hundred and one questions while I pick at the food. Mostly about Flynn, and about Best Bites, but they have some questions about my trip too. I answer most of them, but when they start asking about my unplanned stay in Chesterton, I avoid saying too much. It's not that I won't tell them what happened eventually—Flynn will make sure of that—it's that I need a good night's sleep before I even begin to tackle the feeling of loss I've been pushing down these past thirteen hours.

Since catching my last glimpse of Matt standing in the parking lot of the Hilton Garden Inn.

-

"Morning," Mom chirps when I pad into the kitchen in my pj's.

I slept a solid eight hours but woke up disoriented and missing Matt. Ridiculous that after spending only a couple of days together, his absence already feels like a painful void. I almost indulged in a little pity party for one when I heard the high-pitched chatter coming from downstairs.

A quick visit to the bathroom and a splash of cold water on my face, and I went in search of my daughter.

"Mommy!"

My baby is sitting cross-legged on the counter, her hands stuck in a big bowl of dough.

"Morning, Peanut," I mumble, kissing the top of her head. "What are you up to?"

"Seaman bums. I helped," she informs me with a big smile.

"Cinnamon buns?" I grin at the enthusiastic bounce of her head. "Yummy."

"Yummy," she echoes.

Mom hands me a cup of coffee and waves me to the table. "Sit. These'll be in the oven in a jiffy. Flynnie is being a great help."

"I can see that." My daughter has dough stuck to the front of her shirt, her face, and most of the counter around her. "Where's Dad?"

"At the bakery." Her answer is short and I see a shadow slide over her face.

"What time did he leave?"

"Three. Damn fool got all of three hours sleep. I'm going to have to physically go kick him out of there, or he'll stick around 'til closing time."

"I'll talk to him tonight," I promise. "Starting tomorrow, I'll be the one heading in early."

Mom snorts as she takes the bowl from Flynn and dumps the dough out on the floured counter. "Good luck with that. It's gonna take more than a talk to keep him away. I finally got him to hire extra help, with Christmas orders piling high, but he still insists being there to supervise."

"I'll talk to him," I repeat. "And if I have to I'm not averse to using threats or blackmail." That puts a little smile on Mom's face, but the strain on her is obvious.

Dad is a proud, stubborn man, but he has a few soft spots: the biggest one is his granddaughter.

We spend the morning putzing around. I'm doing laundry while Mom is busy getting on top of her bookkeeping. I'm just moving the last load from the washer to the dryer when Mom sticks her head into the laundry room.

"Who's this *man* Flynnie keeps asking for?"

I knew Flynn would eventually spill the beans, I just hoped I'd have another twenty-four hours or so to let the hurt scab over.

"Matt. It's Matt, but Flynn keeps calling him Man." I recognize the hopeful flare in my mother's eyes. She never says anything, but I know she was disappointed when I announced I was going to raise Flynn by myself. Despite her open mind, she still carries traditional values. She'd like nothing more than to see me settled with a good man. It burns that I'll have to let her down. Again.

"Let's put on a fresh pot of coffee for this." She grabs my hand and pulls me into the kitchen.

Installed at the kitchen table, with my hands folded around a warm cup of java and a gentle prompt from Mom, I tell her everything. Well, almost everything.

"He sounds like a good guy, honey. So why walk away? Is it because he's younger than you are?" Mom covers my fingers that have been plucking at the tissue I needed halfway through my story. Her eyes are warm and understanding, and I fight off another wave of sadness.

"Maybe at first, but in the end, it was just all…complicated."

"Why?"

I roll my eyes at her persistence. "For one thing, we live in different cities. It would be too inconvenient."

"What kind of reason is *inconvenient*? Besides, didn't you tell me last month you were thinking of moving up the coast?" Trust Mom to remember every conversation we've ever had verbatim.

"I was just toying with the idea."

"So? Toy a little harder."

"Okay, but then there's the fact I have a busy life: a business I'm responsible for, a child I'm raising on my own. I don't know how I could make time for a relationship. And Flynn—what if things don't work out? Look at how attached she's grown, in just a few days. What if after a couple of months he decides it's not working out? She would be devastated. And then there's the situation with Dad. There's so much going on in my life right now, it's overwhelming. I can't even begin to—"

"Montana," Mom interrupts my verbal diarrhea with a soft admonishing tone. "Take a breath, honey."

"I'm just—"

She gives my hand a firm squeeze. "A breath, sweetheart." I do as she says, take a deep breath and then another, while she nods encouragingly. "Good. Now let's deconstruct for a minute, and please correct me if I'm wrong. You hired a business manager so you could delegate, right?" I nod. "And you mentioned how amazing this Matt was with Flynn, jumping in, putting her to bed and all that?" I nod again. "You're here now to help us out and find solutions for the bakery, but that's only temporary. Once we have a plan in place, you won't have to worry about us."

"Yeah, but—"

"Hang on, I'm not done." I feel ten years old being made to sit through one of Mom's lectures, but

I let her continue just the same. "I know you prefer holding all the strings in hand, but you're also smart enough to know you can't control everything, no matter how hard you try. Take this from someone with a little more life experience than you; all good things come with risks attached. I can't tell you if this man will stick—no one can predict the future—but I can tell you with certainty that unless you open yourself to the possibility, you will never find out. And wouldn't that be an absolute waste?"

I let her words sink in. It's not news to me that my mother is wise, but her insight still surprises me. Unfortunately, there is one bit of indisputable reality I didn't bring up yet.

"He didn't stop me."

"What was that, honey?" Mom leans in as if she hadn't heard.

"Matt—he never made an effort to stop me. In fact, he practically told me he saw no future."

"Hmmm." She leans back in her chair and takes a sip of her coffee. "Who's to say he's not thinking the same about you right now?"

My initial reaction would be to deny, but instead, I let my thoughts drift back to the last few interactions we had. Could it be I jumped to the worst conclusions, like some self-fulfilling prophecy?

The shrill ring of the phone jerks me from my thoughts, as I watch Mom rush to take the call. She's barely said hello when her face pales and a chill fills my blood.

"Where to?—Okay, I'm on my way."

"Dad?"

She turns at the sound of my voice, pressing her hand to her chest. "They're taking him to St. Luke's."

CHAPTER TEN

Matt

I'm not sure what to expect when I pull up to the simple house I grew up in.

The past few days, I've only briefly spoken to Leena once, but that was before we got stuck in that snowstorm. I haven't been able to connect since then. I'm hoping she's home.

The plan had been for her to wait until the very last minute to inform my parents I'd be home for Christmas, but I wonder if she perhaps spilled the beans early.

The house is quiet and mostly dark, even though it's only eight thirty or so.

The place never was much to look at. I remember we'd paint the siding and porch every five years, but there was never any effort at making it look like a home. Functional was good enough, both inside and outside. Flowers were considered frivolous and the only things growing in the garden during the spring and summer months were vegetables.

The only reason I can tell my folks are ready for Christmas is the Star of David lights hanging in each of the windows.

Christmas is a big religious holiday in their church. As kids, the highlight was always the family meal immediately following long hours sitting in church pews on Christmas morning. No gifts, no Christmas movies or music, and—other than a nativity set next to a large candle sitting on the sideboard every year—no decorations either. A Christmas tree was too much of a mess, no matter how much I begged for one each year.

I just about jump out of my skin when I hear a knock at my driver's side window.

I almost don't recognize her. The last time I saw Leena she was a gangly, awkward teen with big green eyes that were too large for her thin face, and looked older than they should at only thirteen.

This woman is gorgeous, her long dark hair hanging in a thick braid over her shoulder, and her curves barely hidden by the frumpy clothes. The only thing unchanged are those big green eyes. Even at now twenty-five years old, they still look like those of an old soul.

I slip from the car and try to give her a hug, but she pushes me away.

"Father may be watching."

At her whispered words, I spot a slight movement from the corner of my eye and just catch the curtain on one of the upstairs rooms slip back in place.

"I don't care," I state, firmly closing her in my arms. Her arms tentatively slip around my waist, hands grabbing hold of my winter coat.

"You shouldn't have come here," she mumbles, and this time when she moves back I let her go.

"What did you expect? I haven't been able to get hold of you. Are you all right?" I try to look her in the eyes, but she keeps them downcast, shuffling her feet in the traces of snow on the shoveled driveway.

"She found my wish list."

"Mother?" She nods sharply. "What wish list?" I want to know.

"I was so excited, I started making a list of all the things I want to do when we get to Portland." I don't even need to ask all the things she would have on that list, I imagine they're mostly the same things I couldn't wait to enjoy when I left home. "I told them the truth. That you were coming to visit for Christmas, and I was hoping to go back with you after."

"How did they react?"

"Father didn't say anything, hasn't spoken to me at all, but mother dragged me to church. I've been on my knees, praying for forgiveness for two days straight."

If it were up to me, I'd bundle her in my vehicle and start driving, but it's not. It's up to her. I can honestly say my life is better without my parents in it, but just because I don't like them much doesn't mean

I don't still love them. Leena has lived with them longer, and she hasn't had a chance yet to see how families are supposed to function. As much as I'd like to make the call for her, she has to be the one to make the decision.

"You're not welcome here," my father's booming voice sounds from the front porch. When I turn to face him, he's already coming down the steps toward us. "Leena, go inside. Your mother is waiting."

"You're an adult, Leena. You don't have to listen. You have choices," I tell her softly, ignoring my father, who has stopped halfway down the path and is watching.

Leena's eyes dart back and forth between. "I didn't want it to be like this."

"I know, honey. Trust me, I know."

"What should I do? I can't go now. I haven't even said goodbye to Mother, and all my things are still inside."

I never fooled myself into thinking this would be easy, but seeing my sister this tormented was something I didn't expect. I get it—more than ever, I get it—after watching Tana and Flynn drive away, feeling torn in two directions myself.

"Come inside, Leena," Father calls out again. "This is your last chance, or the door will be closed to you for good."

Jesus.

"Look," I put my hands on her shoulders and force her to look at me. "Here's what we'll do; I'm going to find a place to sleep, and you call me tomorrow morning and tell me what you want to do. Okay? Do what you need to do and let me know when you're ready. I'll be back in a flash to pick you up."

The relief on her face tells me I made the right decision, giving her a little more time. "Thank you. I'll call." Without another word, she scoots past me, around Father, and up the steps into the house.

"Why do you have to make it more difficult for her?" Even as the words escape my lips, I know they're useless. "Don't you want to see her happy?"

"She was happy." He returns stubbornly. "Until you filled her mind with tales of the big world out there. Tempting her to turn her back on her family, her intended husband, her Church, and her God."

"I *am* her family," I shout back, slapping my hand on my chest. "She doesn't want the man you're trying to force her to marry, and all her Church and her God have done is give you an excuse to control her. She's not happy. She never was. All I want is for her to have the freedom to choose for herself."

He doesn't say anything else, just stands there glaring at me.

I turn and get back behind the wheel, there's nothing for me here. I can't break through those self-righteous beliefs he clings to like gospel, and I certainly won't bend to them. I just hope Leena finds the strength to do what is best for her.

-

It was late last night when I finally fell asleep.

The Golden Gate Motel was the closest place to my parents' house I could find. Not nearly as comfortable as the suite I spent the past few nights in, but at least the room was clean.

What kept me awake was the silence. Knowing it would still be there when I woke up again. Alone in bumfuck Minnesota, feeling rejected times two, and stewing in my own misery.

The feeling is still there when I wake up, but the bright sunlight streaming in motivates me to shake it off and hop in the shower. The small coffee maker in the room only produces half a cup of dishwater after gurgling for half an hour, and I finally give up and head out in search for stronger stuff.

I find a coffee shop in Cloquet, that serves a very casual breakfast, and I take a drive along the St. Louis river after. Killing time. I hate not knowing what to expect, and the prospect of having to make that fucking drive back to Portland by myself is not sitting well. However, the longer it takes for Leena to call me, the likelier it is she is having second thoughts about coming.

Who the hell am I kidding? Yes, I'm anxiously awaiting Leena's call, but I've been pining for that damn phone to ring since I entered my number into Tana's contact list yesterday morning.

When it finally rings, and I hit answer on my hands-free system, I don't know whether to be relieved or disappointed it's my sister on the phone.

"I want to stay." My heart sinks at her words, but just as I'm about to question her, she adds, "At least until after Christmas. It's only four days away."

"Okay. That's fine, it's what you wanted to do in the first place, right?"

"Right. Except…"

"Except what?"

"I'd hoped we could have a meal together—as a family—but Father doesn't want you here. I'm sorry," she adds in a whisper.

"That's all right." My words are meant to comfort her, but they do little for the sharp stab of disappointment.

This is why I didn't bother coming back for so many years; why would I willingly subject myself to the pain of repeated rejection?

"But what are you going to do for Christmas?" she asks.

Fuck if I know, but to her I say, "Don't worry about me, I'll figure it out. Just give me a call when you're ready."

I've barely hung up the phone when it rings again.

"Did you forget something?"

"………"

"Hello?"

"Matt?" The breath I've been holding whooshes from my lungs at the sound of Tana's voice.

"Tana, it's so good—" I start, but she doesn't let me get very far.

"Matt, I need your help."

CHAPTER ELEVEN

Tana

"Give me twenty minutes."

That's all he says before ending the call.

I prop a sleepy Flynn a little higher on my shoulder and sit down on the hard plastic chair in the lobby, with a view of the parking lot, to wait.

When we arrived at the hospital, we were told Dad was just being taken into the OR, but little else. Mom was invited to wait in the small surgical waiting room, but I was informed no children under twelve were allowed. I urged Mom to go ahead, I would figure something out, and watched her head down the hall. She'd aged at least ten years in the past half hour, and I'd never seen her that fragile. It shook me to my core.

Finding a quiet spot to make some phone calls, it occurred to me my support system was back on the East Coast. Friends I could call on, Mrs. Daily next door, they were all fifteen hundred miles away. There was only one person I could think of I would trust with my daughter.

Flynn is fast asleep when I see Matt's tall shape jogging through the remaining layer of snow toward the entrance, and I want to cry with relief. His eyes scan the lobby and spot me easily. Without a word, he sits down and pulls both me and Flynn into his arms.

"I've got you, sweetheart," he mumbles in my hair, pressing a kiss there. "Go look after your mom. I'll hang out here with the little one."

"You should grab the stroller from the back of the Toyota. She'll sleep in that. She's had breakfast but didn't eat much for lunch, and—"

He cups my face in his cold hands and leans his forehead to mine. "I've got it. Give me Flynn and your car keys and go be with your mom."

His warm brown eyes look at me with such care, I feel overwhelmed and am about to lose the battle with my tears. Brushing away a stray one with his thumb, Matt leans in to press a soft kiss on my lips. Then he easily transfers my sleeping daughter into his hold, and with a tilt of his head, urges me to go.

"Anything?"

Mom looks up when I walk in, her eyes red-rimmed and her hands wringing the life out of the hanky in her lap. She's the only person I know who still carries around a linen hanky.

"Nothing. Where's Flynnie?" she asks, looking behind me.

"She's taken care of. Why don't I go ask if there's anything more they can tell us."

She gives me a nod and a watery smile.

Outside in the hallway, I latch on to the first official looking person I see, a woman wearing surgical scrubs.

"I'm sorry, is there anyone who can tell me what's happening with my father? All my mother and I were told is that he was brought here and was taken to surgery, but we don't even know for what."

"What's your father's name?"

"Maxim Romer."

"Have a seat in the waiting room. I'll find out for you."

True to her word, not ten minutes later, the woman walks in and sits down across from us. "Mrs. Romer?" Mom nods and grabs my hand. "Your husband was brought in suffering a myocardial infarction, or heart attack, from what looks to be an arterial blockage. He is in the care of one of our best cardiologists, Dr. Lockett, who is performing an angioplasty. That's a fairly routine intervention to clear the blockage and restore blood flow to the heart. He'll insert a catheter into an artery, most often in the groin, and guide it to the blocked vessel to clear it. It's likely that a small wire mesh stent will be placed at the same time, to ensure the passage stays open."

"Will that solve the problem?" I ask.

"The immediate problem likely so, but it won't prevent other arteries from clogging up. Dr. Lockett will go over everything with you."

"How long will he be?" Mom wants to know.

"Shouldn't be much longer."

Just as she said, the cardiologist walks in, just twenty minutes after she left, to inform us that Dad is in recovery and will be moved to the ICU shortly. He'll likely have to stay for a few days, but the doctor promises Mom he'll do his best to have him home before Christmas. With a promise to send for her as soon as Dad is in the ICU, he rushes off.

"Now what?" Mom says, her shoulders slumping. "These last few days are going to be crazy at the bakery. I don't know—"

"I'll take care of it."

"But Flynn—where is she anyway?" I knew it wouldn't be long before she got back to that.

"Matt has her."

"Matt? *The* Matt? The one you told me about this morning?"

I shrug. "He told me to call him if I needed him for anything. I needed him for Flynn. He's good with her."

Mom scrutinizes me. "And he just came?"

I nod, a little smile pulling at my mouth. "Took him twenty minutes."

"Wow," she says, her eyebrows raised.

"Yeah. Wow."

-

"Hi."

Matt turns his head at the sound of my voice.

I find him sitting in the cafeteria, drinking coffee, with Flynn still sleeping in the stroller by his side.

"Hey, can I get you something?" he asks when I bend down to check on my daughter.

"I'd do anything for a coffee."

"Coming right up."

I sit down and watch him weave his way through the tables to the counter before turning my gaze outside. At some point, it started snowing again. Lightly this time. I should probably call the bakery and let them know what's going on, but I need to come up with some kind of plan first.

Looks like Dad will be in the hospital at least for the next couple of days, and Mom should stay with him. That's why I told her I'd take care of things, which would normally not be a problem, except for Flynn. Maybe I can set up a cot in Dad's little office off the bakery in the back. I could just bring her in and she could take her naps there. Not ideal to have a toddler underfoot during crunch time, but it is what it is.

"What are you thinking so hard about?" Matt walks up, a tray perched on one hand.

"You look like a pro," I comment, distracting him.

"I am a pro," he retorts with a grin, as he places the tray on the table. "That's what eighteen years of experience does."

"That's a lot of food," I point out when I look at the collection of pastries alongside my coffee.

"You need to eat." He waits for me to take a bite of a Danish. "Now, how's your dad?"

"Dad had a heart attack. Mom's with him now. Only one person allowed in the ICU." By the time I finish explaining what the cardiologist told us, I'm working on a chocolate croissant. I'm a stress eater.

"I'm so sorry," he says, putting a comforting arm around my shoulders. That's when I realize there are tears rolling down my face.

Dropping the now soggy, half-finished croissant back on the plate, I turn my face into his warm neck, indulging in a few moments of weakness. He's quiet, just rubbing a hand up and down my spine. It's exactly what I need.

"Shit. I have to call the bakery," I blurt out, pulling out of his arms. I'd forgotten about that. "That's what I was trying to plan. The place is crazy busy these next few days. *Crap*. I also need to find Flynn a cot. I should—"

"Slow down for a second. I've got nowhere to be the next few days. I'm not a baker, I'm half decent in the kitchen, but I've got years of experience with demanding customers."

I lean in and surprise him with a firm kiss on his lips. "Thank you for that, but the store is not the big concern, the bakery is. Pete's been with my parents for years and takes care of the day-to-day baking, but he can't handle the high pace of the Christmas rush. They just hired a second guy not long ago, but this'll be his first Christmas, so he'll need supervision. When you caught me thinking earlier, I was trying to sort out logistics."

"Are you talking about Flynn? I can look after her," he offers straight away. "Your call, but I can help out while I'm doing that. It wouldn't be the first time I serve customers with a little one on my hip." He notices my questioning look and chuckles. "Not mine: Syd and Gunnar's little boy."

"You have a way with kids," I observe. "Makes me wonder why you don't have any of your own yet." I figure I've said something wrong when I catch the brief clench of his jaw. Putting a hand on his arm, I quickly add, "That sounded like I was prying. I didn't mean to."

His gaze turns to me, and although his mouth smiles, the shadow is not quite gone from his eyes.

"I didn't think you were prying, but that's a subject for another day."

"So noted." His response is not a brush off, but it makes me even more curious.

"We were talking about Flynn," he gently prompts.

"Yes, if you are sure you don't have anything better to do than look after a toddler, it would help out tremendously."

"Consider it done. I'll just grab her seat from your car. She can come with me to pick up my stuff from the fleabag motel I stayed at last night. I'll find something closer by."

There's a lot of information in that statement, but I'm guessing that's probably a subject for another day as well.

"You can take the spare room at Mom's. I'll bunk with Peanut."

Matt

Flynn chatters all the way to the Golden Gate Motel.

She had me in a puddle earlier, when she woke up, rubbed her eyes, and spotted me. Her little face split open in a smile so bright, I thought someone had turned on all the lights.

I don't understand half of what she says, but find she's satisfied with my occasional grunt by way of response.

Parking in front of the dusty motel office, I lift her from her seat and carry her inside, perching her on my hip. The woman behind the desk looks at Flynn suspiciously and fries me with a nasty glare, when I tell her I'll be checking out right away. I'm positive she's already on the phone with the cops by the time I get to my room. It takes me two minutes to throw my stuff in the bag, toss it into the back, and strap a surprisingly pliant Flynn back into her seat.

Best to make tracks, the last thing we need today is for me to get pulled over by the local yokels with someone else's little girl in my back seat.

-

"You must be Matt," the gray-haired woman sitting at the kitchen table says, cool as a cucumber.

Never mind I just let myself into her house with the key Tana handed to me, along with directions.

Convinced I didn't have law enforcement on my tail, I ended up stopping at a diner to get some food into Flynn and myself before taking her home.

"Gramma!" the little girl squeals in my arms, and the woman's face brightens with a smile. She gets up and walks toward me.

"I'm sorry, Tana gave me—"

"Hush," she admonishes, holding out her arms for Flynn, who easily lets herself be transferred. "Montana mentioned you'd show up here. She went to the bakery and dropped me off so I could grab a few things. They've taken Max back to run a few tests. That's my husband—Tana's father." I nod my understanding.

"How is he?" I ask, following her into the kitchen where she sits back down at the table. With practiced ease, she peels the toddler from her snowsuit and with a kiss pressed to the top of her head, sets Flynn down on the floor. The toddler heads straight over to the living room, where a collection of toys is strewn over the floor.

"Sit," she orders, pointing at a chair, before answering with a sigh, "As well as can be expected, I guess. They're checking to see the extent of damage to his heart muscle. If this, whatever the hell test it is, comes back okay, he may be able to come home on Monday. Just in time for me to kick his ass for Christmas." Her eyes sparkle as she looks at me and I let out the snort of laughter I was trying to hold back. I think I'm going to like Mrs. Romer. "You laugh, but I'm not kidding. That man is too stubborn for his own good. He should've been more careful, especially after he got his last warning, and he deserves every kind of abuse I plan for him."

I'd almost be worried for the man if I didn't see the worry on her face and the sheen of tears in her eyes. I'm not sure how to respond. Saying I'll keep my fingers crossed seems hardly appropriate for the occasion. So instead I repeat my earlier, "I'm sorry."

"Never you mind me." Mrs. Romer waves her hand before pushing herself up out of the chair. "Let me show you the bedroom upstairs, and then I'll be heading back to the hospital."

"No need. I'm sure I can find my way," I assure her. "And thank you for putting me up. I could have easily grabbed a hotel, but—"

"Nonsense. I put clean sheets on the bed before Tana got here… My God, that was just last night."

I watch as she almost distractedly shrugs on the winter coat that was tossed over the back of a chair. "Mrs. Romer? How are you getting to the hospital?"

"Driving. My car is in the garage."

Before she has a chance to object, I have my jacket zipped up again, and hoist Flynn in her snow outfit.

"Come on—I'll drive you."

She doesn't say a word until I pull out of the driveway.

"Thank you, Matt."

"No problem."

"You're a keeper."

CHAPTER TWELVE

Tana

"Coffee?"

I almost jump out of my skin when I walk into the kitchen. I haven't had much sleep since finally rolling into bed at eleven last night. Four hours at most.

"*Jesus*, you scared me." Matt—whom I did not expect to see in my mother's kitchen at three in the morning—grins as he slides a travel mug across the counter toward me. "What are you doing up?"

He shrugs, taking a sip of his own brew. "Didn't sleep much."

"How come?"

I watch him set down his coffee and, with his eyes on me, round the counter. "Because," he says in a low voice, as he wraps me tight in his arms. "You were sleeping on the wrong side of the wall."

I didn't get home last night until almost ten, after Mom finally kicked me out of Dad's hospital room. That's where I ended up straight after finishing up at the bakery. I'd called Matt, who assured me Flynn was fine—already tucked in bed after the chaotic day—and suggested I go see my parents. He'd been waiting for me with a glass of wine when I got in, and when I started dozing off, he shooed me off to cuddle up with Flynn. I don't think my head quite made it to the pillow before I fell asleep, my daughter's warm body tucked close.

Matt, who's been an absolute godsend looking after my Peanut, is also looking out for me. I tighten my arms around him, absorbing his calm confidence for what is sure to be a frantic day ahead.

His hand tags my ponytail, pulling my head back. His kiss is sweet, soothing, and I moan in his mouth. A long soak in the tub is usually my method of relaxation, but it doesn't even come close to the limp noodle effect his kiss has. I actually whimper when he releases my lips, making him chuckle.

"Come on, woman, those yule logs won't bake themselves."

I growl, not looking forward to making the sixty-something yule logs before noon today. It's Dad's prized recipe, involving white chocolate and amaretto, and has become quite popular. It's one of my favorite cakes too, but I'm not so sure I'll feel that way tonight.

The chaos in my head is back the moment I get behind the wheel. Traditionally the Saturday before Christmas is, without fail, the busiest day of the year at the bakery. The thought my father won't be there to wave his scepter—as he's done faithfully for the past almost fifty years—is more than unsettling. It's terrifying.

Pete and the new guy are already up to their elbows in batter when I walk in. "Morning."

Both heads turn and echo back, "Morning."

"How's the old man?" Pete asks and I grin. Pete's almost as old as Dad.

"He was sleeping when I got there last night, but Mom tells me apparently the damage to the heart was moderate. Whatever the hell that means. The cardiologist made it abundantly clear; he'll need to make some serious lifestyle changes."

"Bet that went over well. Would've paid good money to have been a fly on the wall for that conversation." The old coot chuckles at his own joke.

"What will happen to the bakery?" the new guy, Paul, asks.

The store staff's been having a heyday teasing these two: Peter and Paul. Pete lets it roll off his back, like he does most things, but Paul hasn't quite found his place yet and is clearly not used to a bunch of women ribbing him. His insecurity shows in the question.

"Well, I'm pretty sure my dad would rise like Lazarus at any discussion around selling. I know him well enough to know he'll want to keep Romer's Bakery on the store window at all cost." With my apron tied and my hair tucked in a hairnet, I slide the first massive jelly roll tray of cake toward me and start drizzling it with amaretto. "The best solution, for now, would be to find someone with both business expertise and baking skills, who can manage both the store and the kitchen."

I'm so focused on what my hands are doing, I don't notice the men have fallen silent at first. When I look up they're both looking at me.

"What?"

"You know you just described yourself, yeah?"

I shake my head at the observation. "Not happening, Pete. I have a business that is on the cusp of expanding nationwide. I've built a life in the Boston area. I have a child. This place is my father's life. He never wanted anything else. I don't want to take over his dream, I never did. I've worked hard for long years so I could live my own dream."

When he's quiet for a moment, I fully expect him to come back swinging. He's never made it a secret he thought I was crazy for heading out on my own.

"You know old Max is crazy proud of you—of what you've built—right?"

His words throw me for a loop. I know Dad loves me to distraction, but he's never come out and said anything about being proud. I always thought he was still disappointed I wasn't going to follow in his footsteps, especially after some of the doozies we had arguing when I was younger. Oh, he asks about Best Bites, but never does much more than nod and grunt.

I don't bother with a response, I'm sure the stunned look on my face says enough.

"Mommy!"

I'm covered in icing and powdered sugar, putting the finishing touches on the final ten logs, when Flynn comes toddling in from the back of the store.

"Hey, Peanut." I smile, lifting her up in my arms and twirling her around.

"Cake?" Her eyes are big as she zooms in on the huge counter covered in yule logs.

"That's grown-up cake, but I'm sure we can find you something you can have after you eat lunch."

"We just had lunch." Matt's deep voice sounds behind me, just as Flynn's sharp eyes spot a dollop of icing clinging to my arm. Before I can stop her, she's scooped it up with her deft little fingers that immediately disappear in her mouth. "Apparently not enough," he adds dryly.

I lift my gaze and meet his warm brown eyes, sparkling with amusement. "Here…" Grinning, I hand her off to him, "…Let me clean up before she makes a meal out of me."

I'm momentarily distracted by the swift, familiar way Matt handles my daughter, perching her easily on his hip with one hand, while grabbing her sticky one with the other before she can get icing all over him. Tearing myself from the domestic picture they make, I head for the large sink at the back, and clean up as best I can, before returning with a wet cloth for Flynn's hand.

"Hi." I'm not sure why I suddenly sound like a starstruck teenager.

"Hello yourself," Matt grins down at me, holding up a bag from Northern Waters Smokehaus at the base of Minnesota Avenue on the point. "Did you know your daughter loves pickles? She ate two massive ones along with a bit of smoked salmon." He shivers, making me chuckle.

"I gather you don't share her tastes?"

"Loved the salmon, but whoever came up with the outrageous idea to stick cucumbers in vinegar should be committed. According to your daughter, you love those abominations too, so I had them stick two in with your sandwich as well. I'm going to seriously have to reconsider kissing you," he rants, and I laugh out loud when he twists his face in a disgusted grimace.

"You'd better kiss me before I eat then," I tease, amazed at the way his eyes instantly radiate heat as he lowers his head.

With his lips on mine, I easily forget where I am, until I hear Pete clear his throat behind me.

"And who might this be?"

Matt

If I didn't know Tana's Dad was hooked up to machines in the hospital, I'd have bet the old man standing behind her, with a grim scowl on his face, was her father.

"Pete—right," Tana mutters cutely, a blush on her face. "Matt, this is Pete Renshaw, he's worked here almost since my parents took over the bakery. Pete," she pointedly says to the guy. "This is Matt Savela. He's my…um…"

"Boyfriend," I finish for her, sticking out my hand. I pretend not to notice the roll of her eyes, or the hostile vibe I get from Pete, who finally clasps my hand in a death grip.

Without moving his glare from me, he addresses Tana. "Is your father aware you have a *boyfriend?*" There's no mistaking the disdain in his voice.

"Pete!" Tana admonishes. "I'm a forty-four-year-old single mother. I've stood on my own two feet for a few decades now. I think I can handle my own love life, thank you very much."

The ensuing stare-off between the two is downright uncomfortable and even Flynn starts wiggling in my arms.

"Right," I decide to break the tension. "Now that's out of the way, Tana, you need to eat something. I doubt you've stopped for food at any point. And Pete, I came to see if I can lend a hand with anything. I'm sure you can set me up."

Five minutes later, Tana is holed up in the small office, eating lunch and being entertained with the little one's happy chatter, and I have been relegated to the large sink with a trolley full of caked-on baking trays, giant mixing bowls, and an assortment of kitchen utensils. *Fun.* Pete is guffawing over by the ovens with the other guy, who was introduced to me as Paul.

I try hard to ignore them as I go to work. It's not like I've never done kitchen clean up before.

"Where's Flynn?" I ask Tana when I stack the last of the clean baking trays on the rack.

"Asleep on a pile of coats on the floor in the office. She almost dozed off with her face in the kolache she was helping me fill."

"I need another tray of challah," one of the girls working in the store calls out, sticking her head in the door.

"I'll get it," I tell Tana, who starts wiping her hands on her apron.

The productivity in this kitchen is crazy. Almost as fast as the two guys were putting trays of baked goods in the cooling rack, they disappeared into the store.

Grabbing a sheet with the shiny braided loaves of bread, I walk into the store, which is even busier than when I walked through a few hours ago. Two young girls and an older woman are behind the counter. The girls helping customers while the woman mans the single cash register.

"Stack them on the empty shelf above the dinner rolls," she calls out when she spots me. "Make it look pretty."

I have no idea what constitutes pretty, unless it comes with lush lips and a bodacious ass, but can certainly try. With a nod, I turn to the shelf and start stacking the loaves.

"Pretty enough?" I ask, catching the woman's eye; she then proceeds to roam up and down my body.

"It is from where I'm standing," she flirts with a wink. The two young girls snicker. "Always knew Tana had good taste. The name's Cheryl. I'd shake your hand but I've been handling bills all day and you never know where those've been." She wiggles her eyebrows and I crack a smile. She's a character.

"Nice to meet you, Cheryl, I'm Matt."

"Oh, honey, I know," she says, before turning to her next customer.

I'm still grinning when I walk into the kitchen.

"What's funny?"

I put my arm around Tana's neck and pull her toward me, dropping a kiss on the top of her head. "I think I was just eye-mauled by your staff. That woman scares me a little."

"Cheryl?" She snorts a laugh. "All bark but no bite. The fact you're still breathing tells me you meet her approval."

"Good to know." I eye the single tray of pastries she has left to fill. "How much longer to finish that?"

"The kolache? Maybe five minutes, why?"

"How about you call it a day after that? Take Flynn and go see your parents. Kids are allowed in the Cardiology Department."

"How do you know that?"

"Because I called this morning. Managed to get your mother on the phone, who says your father is doing well, but wants to see his girls."

I watch as her eyes mist over. "You are so earning brownie points," she teases through the emotion on her face. "But I can't leave. Sugar cookies are next, and even though no one handles a piping bag like Mom, I'm the only one who'll do a half decent job."

"I guess my reputation hasn't reached Boston yet," I joke. "I'm a master with a decorating tip." I hear the two men snort behind me, and clearly, Tana is not buying into it. Don't blame them, my only experience with decorating is when Dino, our chef at the restaurant, asks me to help him plate. I do a mean mashed potato rosette or dressing drizzle, though. How hard can it be?

"He's right. You should get out of here." Pete unexpectedly comes to my aid. "Take your girl and get out of here. Tell the old man to get his ass better, we'll manage with the boy."

The boy, clearly is a slight at me, but I don't give a fuck as long as Tana gets a break.

It takes a few more minutes of reassuring her before she capitulates, but she shows her gratitude with a big hug for Pete and a whispered promise in my ear for 'later.'

Pete turns to me with a grin when the door closes behind them. "Gonna put you to work, boy."

I have no doubt, but that grin disappears fast when he inspects my sugar cookies a couple of hours later.

"Jesus have mercy. Have you got your holidays scrambled in that large head of yours? This ain't Halloween."

Okay, so I still claim I do an awesome potato rosette, but my sugar cookie snowflakes are a little challenged.

They look more like spiderwebs.

CHAPTER THIRTEEN

Tana

"Was your Dad awake?"

I've just come downstairs from putting Flynn down for the night when Matt walks in. I can't help the bark of laughter when I spot the net still covering his hair. Automatically his hand comes up, encounters the thin elastic, and rips the thing off his head, leaving his hair sticking out every which way.

"Pete's an asshole," he mutters, stomping into the kitchen and tossing it in the garbage. "I knew something was up when he waved goodbye with that damn smirk on his face."

"Are you hungry?" I ask, changing the topic.

"Starving. A person can only eat so many sugar cookies." A grumbling Matt is kind of cute. I've not seen him disgruntled like this before and it's almost endearing.

"How did it go with the sugar cookies?"

He looks at me with one eyebrow raised. "I decorated every last one of them. Then I did dishes—again. And I burned my hand taking shit out of the oven—twice." He shows me his injuries and I make appropriately soothing sounds.

"Why don't you sit down? I'll get you something to eat and grab some ointment to put on those burns." I pile a plate high with the spaghetti and meatballs I whipped up when we got back from the hospital. "It's Flynn's favorite," I announce randomly as I set the steaming plate in front of him.

"Mine too," he says, looking up at me with a grin before he stabs a ball on his fork and pops the whole thing in his mouth. "Delicious."

"I'm just gonna grab that stuff from the bathroom."

I quickly scoot up the stairs, mostly to get away from the satisfied moaning sounds Matt is making as he eats. It reminds me too much of the other kinds of sounds I clearly remember him making.

By the time I get downstairs, half his plate is empty. "Give me your hand." I sit down beside him and reach out, checking the blisters on the back of it.

"So how *is* your dad?"

"A grumpy old bear, which means he's feeling better. Mom is sleeping on a cot again tonight. She doesn't want to leave him, she's afraid he'll piss off the nursing staff."

"That's good to hear," Matt rumbles.

I look up at him, raising an eyebrow. "That he's better or that Mom won't be coming home?"

"Both?"

Shoving his chair back from the table, he grabs my hand and pulls me onto his lap, banding his arms around me. I'm pretty sure I was still in pigtails, with a missing tooth or two, the last time I sat on anyone's lap. I feel a little awkward with his eyes at boob level, and mine scanning the top of his head. No bald spots, but plenty of gray. Or is that….

"I think you need a shower," I point out, picking a bit of dried icing from his hair.

"So do you," he counters, a slight twitch at the corner of his mouth.

It takes us two minutes—tops—to get upstairs, naked, and in the shower. His kiss is hungry—with almost voracious intensity—as the water pelts our bodies. Urgent, and needy, I hook a leg around his and grind myself against hard muscle. My fingers dig into the cheeks of his ass, pulling him closer.

"Slow down," he mumbles, releasing my lips. His hand tangles in the wet strands of hair down my back and tugs lightly, forcing me to look up. "I want to savor this." Captivated by his warm gaze, I nod in response, releasing my death grip on his backside and sliding my leg back down.

With gentle hands, he takes his time washing my hair, massaging my scalp, and raking his fingers through the long strands as he rinses it. I stand there, letting him run soapy palms over my skin, leaving goosebumps in their wake.

I'm not a passive person, and it speaks volumes that I quietly let him tend to me. The only thing moving are my eyes, following his movements.

Perhaps I should be concerned I am falling this hard in such a short time, but no man has ever cared for me like this. Not even close.

I watch as he quickly washes his own hair and body, but when his hand lazily strokes his cock a few times; I drop to my knees and without hesitation take him in my hand and mouth. His groan, when my tongue finds the sensitive spot right under the tip, only spurs me on and I take him deep. I watch from under my lashes as he braces himself against the wall. Curving his other hand around my head, he guides me up and down his shaft, his eyes burning into mine.

It doesn't take long before I feel the muscles ripple in his thighs and he abruptly pulls himself free. "I need inside you," he mumbles. He pulls me to my feet and swings me around so my back is plastered to his front. With an arm around my waist—anchoring me—he runs the other hand down the back of my leg, lifting it so my knee is hooked over his forearm, spreading me wide. "On your toes." His whisper is urgent against the shell of my ear.

The next moment he's inside me, hard and deep, the angle reaching parts of me that have my eyes roll back. His hand slides up from my belly to curve around my breast, fingers plucking at my nipple. "Honey," I moan, dropping my head back on his shoulder, as his hips slap against my ass, setting a punishing rhythm.

I'm lost to sensation. His body tightly curved around me, rubbing my back with the rasp of his chest hair. With the rough pads of his fingertips, he sends pulses from my painfully hard peaks straight down to where his cock is pounding my pussy. I gasp for air, suspended in time.

His breath becomes ragged as I feel his body flex behind me. "Touch yourself," he growls, and I immediately slip a hand down, fingers moving furiously over my clit.

The moment his teeth sink into my shoulder I fall over the edge: muscles contracting with the force of my release, as his guttural groan and jerking body signals his.

"Beautiful," he mutters, never letting go when he turns and takes my full weight as he leans his back against the wall.

Still taking care of me.

Matt

"Don't go," I mumble when I feel her getting out of bed.

She'd wordlessly followed me into the spare bedroom after our shower last night, sliding naked under the sheets with me. Exhausted, it didn't take me long to drift off with her soft body pressed against mine.

"I have to," she says softly, leaning down to press a sweet kiss on my mouth. I blink open my eyes and find her smiling at me. "Thank you for taking care of me, and I don't mean just taking over at the bakery yesterday. You were looking out for me, even when I was just a stranger at a gas station." Her hand trails along my scruffy jaw before tracing my lips with her finger. "You keep surprising me at every turn and I fall a little harder each time."

"Montana," I whisper against her fingers, but she shakes her head sharply.

"There are so many uncertainties: my father's health, the future of the bakery, my own business—and last, but definitely not least, there's you. I'm not quite sure how or where to fit everything, but you make me want to try."

Tagging a hand behind her neck, I pull her down, roll her under me, and kiss her hard.

Fuck, this is crazy.

One by one I've seen my friends back home fall hard—I was happy for every one of them when they found love—I just never believed it was in the books for me.

I was wrong.

"We'll make it work," I promise her, lifting my head to look her in the eye. "I can't tell you where this road is taking us, but I can assure you I don't want to get off."

Her eyes crinkle as she smiles up in my face. "Are we a little crazy?"

"Certifiable." I grin back and give her soft brush of my lips, before rolling off her. "Now get ready for work. Pete will be happy to see you instead of my mug."

Soft laughter trails after her as I follow her naked ass padding into the bathroom. The next second, she pokes her head back out. "I almost forgot. Mom needs a change of clothes. If I pack a bag, do you think you could drop it off at the hospital sometime this morning? I'd do it, but we're doing pies today."

"Sure. We'll be out and about anyway."

"Oh? What are you up to?"

"This and that," I evade with a smirk.

-

"More."

I raise my eyebrow at Flynn, who just inhaled her second pancake almost as fast as she did her first.

"Let's give it a minute, okay? I don't think that second one made it quite down to your tummy yet." I ignore the resulting pout on her lips. She's quite proficient at those, but luckily she's still easy to distract. "So are you gonna help me today?"

"Make chwismiss," she says with a big smile.

"You bet. We have a few things to pick up in town, and I need you to help me wrap presents."

"Wanna wap pwesents."

"Yes, *after* we run a few errands. We'll come back here, wrap some presents, and get ready to surprise Mommy."

"Pwesents for Mommy?"

"Yes, but you can't tell her, because it's a surprise."

"Supwise."

"Exactly." Fucking adorable how she repeats every second word back. I have no idea if she understands the concept of *surprise*, so I'll have to keep a close check on her.

Satisfied I have her sufficiently distracted, I turn to get myself another coffee and pour some batter in the pan for my own breakfast, when I hear her behind me.

"More."

-

"Did you know your granddaughter has a hollow leg or two?"

Mrs. Romer chuckles as I hand her Flynn, holding onto the bag Tana asked me to take to bring over. "Let me guess, you made pancakes for breakfast?"

"I did, actually. She ate three to my four. I couldn't believe it."

"Fwee," Flynn confirms for her grandmother, holding up four fingers. Mrs. Romer bounces the toddler on her hip, before turning back to me.

"I know. She eats like a bird the rest of the time, but when it comes to anything sweet, she gorges herself."

"Are you gonna let me see my granddaughter, or do I have to come out there?"

The gritty voice coming from inside the room must be Tana's dad.

"Hold your horses," Mrs. Romer mutters under her breath, as she rolls her eyes at me before walking into the room. I tentatively follow behind.

"Grampa!" Flynn almost launches herself onto the bed, but Tana's mother manages to hold her back, whispering quietly in her ear before releasing her carefully into her husband's waiting arms. The little girl snuggles into his hold, tucking her tow-colored head under his chin, but all the while his dark glare pierces me to the floor just inside the door.

"Maxim." Mrs. Romer's sharp hiss draws his attention. "This is Matt, Tana's friend. He—"

"I know who he is, woman." He cuts her off before his eyes slide back to me. "Well? Are you gonna stand there shuffling your feet or are you going to come in?"

I'd rather sit my bare ass down in a nest of fire ants than go in, but my feet are moving already. "Mr. Romer," I say, holding out my hand. The scrutiny of the older man feels way too familiar. Much like my father looks at me: with near disdain. It suddenly seems important Tana's dad doesn't weigh and find me lacking, like my own father does.

I hold my ground and finally he grasps my hand, his hold much firmer than I would've expected from a man who just had a heart attack.

"Sit," he bites off before turning to his wife. "You can go have a shower now. Matt can keep me company."

"Man!" Flynn's head bobs up, almost hitting her grandfather on the chin.

"Yes, sweetheart."

"We wap pwesents now?"

"Not yet. We first have to go shopping," I remind her, as she worms from her grandfather's hold to the edge of his bed, where I catch her and prop her in the curve of my arm. Her little hands clap against my cheeks and she butts her nose against mine.

"Soon?"

"Yes, soon." At my promise, she settles on my lap, and I notice Tana's father watching us.

"She likes you," he says, perhaps a little surprised.

"And I like her."

"Hmmm." A pregnant pause follows and I have to work not to look away from his intense stare. "And my daughter—you like her too?" he finally asks.

"I do. She makes it easy."

He hums again and his eyes slide down to his granddaughter, who is playing with my watch. "I'm not sure how long I have left," he says suddenly, barking out a hoarse laugh. "Ironic, isn't it? One moment you put things off, pretending time hasn't passed at all, and the next you stare death in the face, wondering if there's even enough time left for you to settle your affairs."

It's my turn to hum, but I do it understanding what he means. Life is short, so don't put off to tomorrow, what you can do today.

"I don't know you from Adam, and I don't know if you'll stick around," he continues, raising his hand to stave off any assurances I might offer, but his eyes stay glued to a surprisingly quiet Flynn. "But I'm asking you anyway." Finally his gaze meets mine, and instead of the strong judgment I saw before, there is only a silent plea left in his eyes. "I need to know, whatever happens, you'll look after her—after them."

I don't need time to think about an answer, but to show him I take his question seriously, I give it a moment before speaking.

"I absolutely will, and I'm pretty sure you'll be around so I can prove it to you. But just so you know, your daughter is very good at looking after herself."

For the first time since I walked in, I see his mouth twitch as he gives me his seal of approval.

"Good answer."

CHAPTER FOURTEEN

Matt

"Ohmigawd! What's this?"

Shit. I never noticed her car drive up.

I swing around from the potato leek soup I was trying to have ready before rounding up Flynn and putting her to bed. As it is, Flynn is still wide awake, dancing around the living room to the music of some Christmas movie I found on TV. She's a mess: garland draped around her neck and a jaunty red bow she snagged off a present—stuck on her head— hanging lopsided by her ear. I'd counted on having time to clean up a little before Tana walked in.

I'd noticed the lack of Christmas decorations yesterday morning. Not something I was used to myself growing up, but I'd expected a family like Tana's to have at least some. A sweet little thing like Flynn certainly deserved them.

I had planned to ask Mrs. Romer about it earlier, but the encounter with her husband made me forget all about it. That's why it took a little longer to get everything I thought we'd need. Including the tree and a stand.

That proved to be a challenge, trying to get a tree fitted into the base, with a three-year-old under your feet. Never mind bringing it inside. That's when I had my first doubts, while I was trying to figure out where to put the damn thing. It had seemed like such a good idea at the time, but moving someone else's shit around to fit a tree I hauled into their house uninvited, made me reconsider my grand plan. They may not even want one. What if they're Jewish? Tana never mentioned anything and I couldn't see any visual evidence, but I really have no way of knowing for sure.

My enthusiasm turned to concern and I abandoned the tree, for the moment, and focused instead on getting the couple of presents I picked up wrapped. While I was doing that, Flynn got into the bags of decorations I'd picked up at Walmart, and had started on the tree. Still sitting in the middle of the room, three branches at the bottom were now heavy with about twenty-five balls, copious strands of garland, and the plastic Walmart bags they came in.

I didn't have the heart to change anything and with dinnertime come and gone, I focused on that instead. Found a movie on TV and plopped Flynn on the couch.

Apparently that didn't keep either, as I watch the silver garland trail behind her as she dances her way over to her mother, who still stands frozen in the doorway.

Oh, big shit.

Tana

Christmas threw up in our house.

From the corner of my eye, I catch the shocked expression on Matt's face, but I can't tear my eyes from the beautiful Christmas tree in the middle of the living room.

A real tree.

Mom always preferred the ratty old fake one that gets stored in the basement every year, with the decorations still on it. Traditionally she has Dad haul it upstairs on Christmas Eve, while she rushes around to decorate the rest of the house.

Dad and I tried for years to get her to concede to a fresh-cut tree, but while she agreed nothing compares to the scent of fresh pine, she would remind us in no uncertain terms that it would be her vacuuming fallen needles for months after.

But Matt got us a real tree.

"Mommy, we gots chwismiss!"

"I see that, Peanut." I look down at my daughter, who has her arms around my knees, staring up at me with a giant smile. I pluck the haphazard bow from her ear and stick it on top of her head, where I'm sure it started out. "You look beautiful."

Finally I raise my eyes and almost chuckle when I see the apprehensive look on Matt's face.

"So yeah, about that," he says, tilting his head to the tree. "It seemed like a—"

"I come home after a sixteen-hour day, spent sweating in a hot bakery I had to share with a grumpy old man and his nervous sidekick. I'm tired, I'm hungry, I'm gross and sticky—and this is what I find when I walk in the door?" I swing Flynn up in my arms and have to bite my lip not to laugh at his crestfallen expression.

"I…" he starts, but I've teased enough.

"It's perfect," I whisper, walking up to him, my eyes misting over as I slide my free arm around his waist.

His face relaxes as he wraps both me and Flynn in his hold. "Yeah?"

"Yeah. Absolutely perfect. Best way to come home. Bar none."

He bends down and plants a hard kiss on my lips.

"Man!" Flynn calls out, apparently not happy she's not being included, and pats his cheek with her little hand. Matt grins in my face when he pulls away.

"Yes, honey. What's up?"

"Mommy supwise?" He turns to look at the big grin on my face and the single tear rolling down my cheek.

"I think Mommy was very surprised."

-

"Don't go," he mutters for the second time in as many days when I try to roll out of bed.

After a late dinner last night, I'd given Flynn a bath and put her to bed, while Matt cleaned the kitchen. Together we moved the tree into the corner by the window. It's where Mom usually wants her tree, on top of a small sideboard. Matt's tree is much too large, so we had to move the piece of furniture into the dining area.

Matt draped the little white lights he'd bought in the branches, but when he tried to reposition the decorations Flynn had clumped together, I insisted we keep it just as it was.

He'd been asleep by the time I came out of the bathroom. I slipped under the covers and snuggled into his side. His arms immediately curved around me but he never woke up. I drifted off moments later.

"Last day," I softly say, turning to face him. "Half a day, actually. The bakery always closes at two on Christmas Eve and stays closed until after New Year's." I sit up, swing my legs over the edge. "By the way, don't forget to call your sister. Let her know she's welcome here for Christmas if she changes her mind about staying home."

He'd told me about the confrontation with his father in front of his parents' place, and his sister's choice to wait until after Christmas to come home with him. I sympathized; he brushed it off as being nothing less than what he'd expected, but I'd brought it up again last night. I'm not sure why Leena popped up in my mind, but it may have had something to do with Matt's excitement over Christmas. From what I gather, the holiday wasn't exactly a warm and fuzzy affair. Matt mentioned they never had Christmas presents and didn't have a tree growing up either. I couldn't help but think of his sister, who would be missing all of that, so I suggested he try to get in touch with her to make sure everything is all right.

"I'll call her," he promises, burying his nose in my hair when I lean down for a kiss. "What time will they release your dad? I can always pick your parents up."

"Thank you, but they have to wait for the cardiologist to do his rounds, which should be sometime after lunch anyway. I'll head over straight after I close up shop."

"Fair enough. Then how about I take Flynn grocery shopping? Tomorrow's Christmas and we're running on empty. If you bring something for dessert from the bakery, I'll take care of dinner. I can pick up a prime rib roast. I cook a mean one."

I lift my head, and I'm sure every single emotion I feel right now is plastered on my face. "I've been so preoccupied, I hadn't even thought about Christmas dinner." I stroke my fingers lightly down his face, almost testing to make sure he is real. "You're amazing, do you know that?"

Matt

"Not sweepy."

I bite down a grin. Flynn is rubbing her eyes and slurring her words, trying to convince me she's not ready for a nap.

We've been constantly on the go this morning and she's been a trooper. I'm floored how long she lasted, being dragged along in and out of ridiculously busy stores.

The only time she had a little meltdown was when I made the mistake of taking her into a pet store we passed. She fell in love with the puppies and threw a little tantrum when I tried to explain Mommy would probably be upset if we came home with one. In the end, I had to tuck her under my arm and walk to the car, where she promptly quieted down, but not before I'd received a few suspicious glares.

"When you wake up, Grandpa and Granny will be home."

"Fo chwismiss?"

"Sure, they'll be home for Christmas."

"Man?"

"Yes, munchkin."

"Sing."

"You want me to sing?"

"Woowee."

"What?"

"Wittle tiny."

I'm seriously going to have come up with some other material for my repertoire. Somehow I don't see myself singing a Christmas lullaby in the middle of summer.

That is, assuming I'll be around to sing her to sleep in the summer.

I haven't really thought much beyond tomorrow, to be honest. There's too much going on. There are moments I feel like I slipped down the rabbit hole, dropped into someone else's life. It's so far removed from my daily routine—unfamiliar—and yet I enjoy every second of it.

Still, the reality is I came here with a purpose—to help my sister spread her wings—and that involves going back home to Portland. Even if it means I have to leave this little beauty and her mother behind.

Fuck, it'll hurt. It hurts just thinking about it, but Tana will eventually head back home as well, and I'll be waiting.

"Pweeze?" Flynn's little hand pulls at my sleeve.

"Okay. Close your eyes and I'll sing."

I've barely sung a verse and she's asleep. Pulling the covers up to her chin, I press a kiss to her forehead and tiptoe out of the room, pulling the door shut behind me.

Heading downstairs, I pull out my phone. Twice this morning I've tried to call Leena without any luck, and now again there's no answer at the house. Granted, this time of year there is no shortage of church social events or services. It's most likely what they're doing, but I'm still a little uneasy.

I'm just putting the rub I made for the roast in the fridge when the front door swings open.

"It's beautiful!" Mrs. Romer is the first one in the door and she makes a beeline for the tree. I'm surprised, I thought she didn't like real pine. "It actually smells like Christmas in here," she exclaims with a wave of her arm.

"We've been telling you that for years," Mr. Romer grumbles, leaning heavily on Tana's arm. She catches my eye and winks. "I wish I'd known I have to be half dead for you to get one, I would've had a heart attack years ago."

"Oh, hush, old man. It wasn't me who got it. Let's get you out of your coat and settled on the couch."

"Matt got the tree, Dad," Tana fills in. His eyes shoot to me.

"You're still here?"

"Dad!"

"Maxim, behave!"

I bite down a grin when I see one of the old man's eye close in a wink. The old coot likes stirring the pot.

Mrs. Romer, who now insists I call her Betty, seems to be on board with my plan for a roast, sniffing appreciatively at the rub she fished out of the fridge. I get the sense she's not comfortable with me taking over the entire meal, though, so when she says she'll handle the sides, I don't argue.

The afternoon passes quickly, especially once Flynn gets up from her nap. She's wired. Not even a rerun of *White Christmas*—apparently a tradition in the Romer household, which almost succeeds in putting me to sleep—puts a dent in her energy.

"Let's go for a drive, see the lights," I suggest to Tana after an easy meal of leftover soup and sandwiches. "The car ride may knock her out," I add under my breath.

"Head over to Bayfront Park. You remember the giant Christmas tree?" her father asks Tana before turning to me. "Duluth is known for its holiday lights, did you know that?"

"I did, actually. Never had a chance to see them for myself, even though I grew up around here, so this will be a check on my bucket list."

-

Bayfront Park is the first stop, and we actually park the car and walk around. I carry Flynn, and Tana slips her hand in mine. Anyone looking at us would see a family out on Christmas Eve.

Another check on my bucket list. One I never thought I'd be able to scratch off.

By the time we leave the park, Flynn's little head is resting against my shoulder, her eyes almost closed. I drive through a neighborhood Tana points out, but when I'm about to turn down another street and do a quick check of the back seat, I see the little girl is fast asleep.

"Look," I softly prompt Tana, when my phone buzzes in the cupholder. Not wanting to use the handsfree and wake Flynn up again, I quickly pull to the side of the road and answer, startled to hear my sister's voice.

"Matt? I need you to come get me."

CHAPTER FIFTEEN

Tana

It's already closing in on ten thirty when we pull up in the driveway of a rather plain house. There are a few cars parked along the curb on the otherwise quiet street. The only things showing the time of year are the two lit stars hanging in the home's front windows.

Waves of tension are coming off Matt, whose hands have been white-knuckled around the steering wheel. He hasn't said much since he hung up the phone.

"Stay in the car," he says as he gets out, not even waiting for my acknowledgment.

Like hell I will.

Scrambling out of the car, I open the back door, pluck a sleeping Flynn from her seat and turn to the house. Matt is standing halfway down the path, glaring at me with his hands on his hips.

"What the hell do you think you're doing?" he bites off when I reach him.

"If you think that after having my back this past week through every conceivable crisis, I would let you walk into that house alone, you haven't been paying attention. This can't be a relationship where one gives and the other takes—we are either partners in this, or we have nothing."

I stand my ground, even when he growls with frustration and runs his hand through his hair.

"My parents can be cruel. I don't want you exposed to that," he finally whispers.

"From what I gather, your parents are assholes, but that in no way reflects on you. You are the finest man I know, and if your sister is anything like you, I already know I will love her too. Now let's go get her."

I resolutely step around him and march up to the porch, where he stops me with a hand on my arm. Reaching out, he takes Flynn, lifting her onto his own shoulder before he pins me with a dark look.

"Love her *too*?"

It slipped. I was hoping he missed that, but apparently not. "Yeah, well," I sputter. "We'll get to that later."

"Damn right we will," he grumbles, grabbing my hand with his free one as he pulls me up the steps.

A severe looking, older man opens the door. It's not hard to tell where Matt got his looks: the man would be handsome if not for the angry scowl leaving deeply grooved frown marks between his eyebrows. Matt has laugh lines instead, and those make him beautiful.

"Didn't I tell you you're not welcome here?" His rough bark startles Flynn, who lets out a whimper. "You're interrupting a family event. You are no longer considered family."

"I'm not here for you, Father. I'm here for my sister."

"You no longer have a sister." His father steps out on the porch, poking a finger in Matt's face.

It gives me a chance to peek inside where a small group of people is gathered, all looking at the door. The one person who stands out is a young woman in a plain white cotton dress with tears running down her face. Oh, hell no.

"Like hell I don't," I hear Matt fire back, as I quickly slip around the men facing off, and march boldly into the house.

"Leena?" I walk straight up the sniffling girl, ignoring the mumbled protests around me. "You don't know me, my name is Tana and I'm in love with your brother. Do you want to stay here, or do you want to come with us?"

"Leena!" An older woman, who can only be the mother, pushes me out of the way and gets into her daughter's face. "You have a husband waiting for you at the church, don't you dare walk out on your responsibilities. Go with these people and your soul will be soiled. Your God is benevolent to those who live a life of worship and clean of sin, but he will strike you down if you cross him!"

The woman's voice has been rising throughout her tirade, and I've had enough of the religious zealot.

"Do you want to come?" I ask the girl again, sidestepping her mother and holding out my hand. "Matt is waiting outside."

That last addition broke the seal, because she firmly clasps my hand and lets me pull her from the house.

"You leave this house, you'll never set foot here again."

Leena releases my hand and turns to her father. "Your loss."

I would've applauded her comeback, if not for Flynn, who has woken up during the altercation and stares with big eyes and trembling bottom lip at Matt's angry father. Before she can bust loose, I quickly step into her line of sight and put a comforting hand on her back.

"Are you ready to go home, Peanut?"

I try not to react to the derisive snort behind me, as I look up and try to will Matt to turn his eyes to me instead of shooting fire at his father.

"It's a sad excuse of a man who's willing to take another man's rejects for his own." I can feel Matt freeze solid in front of me, as his sister lets out a sharp hiss, but the man is not done yet. "You could've redeemed yourself, you know? Taken on the ministry that was planned for you. A man who can't father offspring is not good for much else in the eyes of the Church."

"That's enough!" I bark, swinging around to face the horrible excuse for a human being, as my poor baby bursts into tears behind me. "I don't care what you call me…" Bouncing on the balls of my feet with fury, I wave my finger in his face. "…but don't you ever call my child a reject. And for the record, Matt is a real man: one who protects, provides for, and treasures those he loves—and that includes my daughter, who is lucky to have him as a strong and loving father figure in her life. Not that you'd recognize one. You can take your Church and shove it up your ass!"

"*Wow*," Leena mutters, as I whip past her and rush down the steps.

I don't want to give that awful man the satisfaction of the tears which start streaming down my face. How on earth a gentle and kind soul like Matt came from these crazy people is beyond comprehension. I climb in the front seat and drop my face in my hands.

Apparently Matt and his sister are not far behind. I hear the car doors open and close but I refuse to look up. I'm embarrassed. I made a scene back there and I fucking hate drama.

Matt

I thought she'd run after getting a taste of the fucked-up nest I sprouted from. For sure after my father decided to let loose on me, dropping a proverbial bomb in the process. It's nothing new for me—even if I haven't heard this tirade since the day I left. Although the words themselves no longer cut me, the intent behind them still does. Especially since his objective was clearly to humiliate me in front of the two people who've become my world. I may not have fathered the little girl who burrows herself against me, looking for safety, but under no circumstances could I imagine treating her the way he does either me or my sister.

The last thing I expected was to see Tana swing around, her face tight with rage, and tear into him— leaving both him and me—for entirely different reasons, at a loss for words.

Leena is the first one to follow Tana when she storms to the car, but I take one last look at my father.

"A real man worships his family before his God, and the love he receives in return is his ultimate reward." Without another word, I turn on my heel.

Flynn is shell-shocked, sniffling quietly when I strap her safely into her seat. I kiss her head and look up to see my sister's wide eyes on us. I give her a wink. When I slide behind the wheel, Tana is crouched over, her face hidden in her hands.

I back away from the house and drive a few blocks before I pull the car over on the shoulder when I hit the county road. Turning off the engine, I put my hand on Tana's back and rub gently.

"My parents didn't believe in vaccinations," I start, my eyes focused on the deserted road ahead. "They would say that we shouldn't stand in the way of God's will, and if we were without sin, God would spare us illness and disease. I was fifteen when I contracted the mumps. I was uncomfortable for a week or so, but it passed. Wasn't until two years later I learned it had more of an impact than I thought." I check the rearview mirror to find Flynn blissfully asleep again, but my sister looks right back at me. She's probably heard the story before, but never from me. Beside me, Tana sits up and I see the tear tracks down her cheeks, but she's not crying anymore. Still, I reach out and brush my thumb under her eye. "Remember you mentioned Beth Oberg and I told you I remembered her?" I wait for her nod. "It's true that my father brought her up as a threat whenever he tried to get me back in line, but what I failed to mention was I actually knew Beth. I'd met her at a church event and was quite taken with her. A couple of years older, she had a defiant edge that attracted me. Not to mention she was built. I lost my virginity to her in the cornfield behind the rectory." Tana reaches for my hand and twines our fingers, giving me an encouraging squeeze. "When she told me a few months later that she was pregnant, I confronted my father, who laughed in my face when I told him I wanted to get married. Beth had a bit of a reputation I hadn't been aware of, and he wanted me checked for venereal diseases by the family doctor. The doc brought up that mumps can, in rare cases, cause sterility in older boys and men. Turns out that baby couldn't have been mine."

"He always said it was God's punishment for your sins," Leena pipes up from the back seat.

"Sure he did," Tana jumps in, turning in her seat so she can look at her. "If only to hide the fact it was his responsibility you guys weren't vaccinated and Matt was able to get mumps in the first place." Sliding back in place, she looks at me and lifts my hand to her lips. "Just for the record: sperm has little to do with fatherhood. Flynn's father wanted nothing to do with her, not before or after she was born. Not everyone is made to be a father…but you are."

Tagging her behind the neck, I lean over and kiss her hard, leaving my forehead resting against hers. "You've got to stop saying that shit in front of Flynn or my sister." With my other hand, I guide hers against my fly so she can feel the state of my cock. "I can't properly thank you with the kids looking on."

"Hey, I'm twenty-five," comes from the peanut gallery.

-

"Aren't you in bed yet?" Tana says, when we walk in the door to find her father still sitting up in his chair.

"How am I supposed to sleep? For all I know you've been kidnapped and hauled off to Canada, never to be heard of again!"

"Maxim!"

I chuckle, the grumbling curmudgeon is growing on me.

"Mom, Dad, this is Leena, Matt's sister. Their parents were trying to marry her off to a man she doesn't much care for. Am I right?" she asks Leena, who looks shell-shocked but manages to nod. She plucks the sleeping toddler from my shoulder. "Right. They're in Esko, and in a pretty fanatical LLC. I'm sure that's explanation enough for now? I've gotta get my kid into bed. We've had a rough night. Leena, wanna come with? I'll grab you some clothes—I'm sure mine will fit you—and I'll show you your room."

"That's my girl," Maxim rumbles, when she disappears up the stairs with Leena behind her.

"Mine now," I challenge him, sitting down on the couch. I expect him to protest, but he just slowly turns to face me and raises his bushy eyebrow into his receding hairline.

"Well, you've got yourself a handful," he concedes.

"Not gonna argue you on that."

"Now, boys," Tana's mother mutters, as she gets up to set another place at the breakfast table.

No questions asked.

This is what family should be.

CHAPTER SIXTEEN

Tana

I wake up to Flynn bouncing up and down on the bed between Matt and me.

Last night, I'd changed the sheets on the bed in the spare bedroom and settled Leena in there with one of my old nightgowns and some clothes to wear. I figured she might need the space to get a hold of her life, which seems to be spinning out of control. Matt and I managed just fine, sandwiching Flynn in the double bed. A little cozy, but the prospect of waking up together on Christmas morning was worth the odd little elbow in my face or heel in my stomach.

The reality is a little less romantic, since I'm in need of at least another two solid hours of sleep, but my daughter clearly has other ideas.

"Chwismiss! Wanna see pwesents."

"Give me a minute, Peanut." I stretch and rub the sleep from my eyes, when there's a soft knock on the door.

"Are you decent?" Mom's voice sounds on the other side and I throw a quick glance over at Matt who, just like me, was smart enough to wear pj's to bed. "I just want to get Flynnie so she can help me with the cinnamon buns."

"Ciman buns!"

"Hey, kiss Mommy first," I protest when my girl starts climbing over me. She giggles and blows a raspberry against my cheek.

"Now, Man."

"Matt, baby, it's Matt."

"Man…t!"

Matt snickers before letting out a loud whoosh when Flynn jumps from my chest to his. He gets the same treatment. When the door opens, and Mom sticks her head inside, Flynn's already climbing off the bed.

"Merry Christmas," she says softly, grinning as she pulls Flynn close. "My present to you is another hour in bed."

I watch until the door closes and then turn to Matt. He's lying on his back, but his head is turned toward me—he's watching me with a soft look on his face.

"What?"

"You love me."

That was coming and there's no reason to deny it, so I nod. "I do. I know it's ridiculously fast, given that we've—"

"Stop," he interrupts, reaching for a strand of hair and giving it a tug. "Given the dog's years worth of crises and drama we lived through in the past eight days, I'd say it's perfect timing. Besides, what does it matter? We're clearly in sync, setting our own pace—since I love you too."

Without losing his eyes, I bridge the space left by my daughter and curl myself around him. His hand lazily strokes my arm laying across his stomach. It's a simple moment—a happy one—until the toilet flushing in the adjoining bathroom reminds me of the complexities of our situation.

"But what now? Where do we go from here? We have lives, responsibilities. Those don't necessarily line up." I know I'm rambling but I'm suddenly scared.

"True," he agrees, turning to his side so our fronts are aligned. He brushes the hair out of my face. "We're doing things a little backward, but Rome wasn't built in a day. We have a few more days to figure things out before I have to head back. I can find Leena and me a hotel room nearby, give you and your parents some space to get a handle on the day-to-day running of the bakery."

"I don't want you to leave."

He tugs me even closer. "I don't particularly want to leave either, but your father is recovering from a pretty major heart attack, and I'm sure your parents don't need a couple of strangers cramping their space. Not with everything going on." My parents might have a thing or two to say about that.

Still, I hate that he makes sense. The last time I pouted was probably a good number of decades ago, but I'm pouting now.

"I see where Flynn got that particular talent," Matt teases, grinning as he rubs a finger over my pursed lips. "Come on. It's our first Christmas together, Leena's very first Christmas the way normal people celebrate. Let's not waste it."

-

The scent of warm yeast and cinnamon greets me when I walk into the kitchen. Flynn is sitting on the counter stirring something in a bowl, sneaking a taste of what I assume is the icing, when she thinks Mom isn't looking. Mom shoots me a wink when she sees me come in. Flynn will learn soon enough that my mother has eyes in the back of her head.

Leena is already up and evidently put to work, since Mom is instructing her how thick to cut the rolled up dough into buns.

"Merry Christmas, everyone."

Three heads turn in my direction, but my attention is on my daughter who is smiling ear to ear, a streak of icing on her cheek.

"We gots pwesents!" She flings the whisk in the direction of the Christmas tree, splattering icing all over the kitchen.

"Peanut—careful!" I grab the gadget from her hand and plunk it in the sink. Immediately her bottom lip starts wobbling but before I can stave off the impending flow of tears, Matt's voice sounds behind me.

"That was the best Christmas welcome I've ever had, little one."

Flynn goes from almost in tears to happy giggles when he steps around me and scoops her up in his arms. That's when I get a good look at his face, which has a large dollop of icing rolling down his cheek.

Matt

"Nonsense."

I look up at the man at the head of the table, my fork halfway to my mouth. Tana's father was the last person I expected to object when I casually mentioned to Leena I managed to find a place for us to stay online.

-

Christmas in the Romer house has been an experience. For one thing, the whole family stays in their pj's until they've unwrapped gifts. I discover why, when apparently everyone receives some new piece of clothing they then change into. Courtesy of Betty, if my guess is right, although I have no clue how she managed to include me and Leena in that tradition. She's been with her husband in the hospital since I met her, and no one knew until last night Leena would be here.

I thought I was the only one with any time to pick up a few things, but as it turns out, Tana's mother spent her time sitting beside her husband's hospital bed well, ordering stuff online and having it delivered to a neighbor.

None of the gifts were excessive, and the red hoodie she got me isn't really my color, but I'll wear that sucker until it falls in threads off my body.

I got Tana's Dad a fly tying kit, Betty a CD of a remastered, limited edition of the 1957 Elvis Christmas Album, and Flynn was over the moon with the simple plastic toboggan. Leena had been little more of a challenge, but I ended up getting her a simple cell phone with earbuds, and loaded it up with music.

I struggled most with Tana's gift. Nothing seemed meaningful enough, but a quick phone call to Syd helped me locate a store in Duluth, where I ended up finding flannel pajama pants in a smaller size. Matching elves and candy canes. Cheesy, I know, and it had been good for a chuckle, but the shimmer in Tana's eyes when she smiled showed me she got my message.

Tana floored me when she gave me a small album. On the first page she had written: For All The Years You Missed. On all the following pages were printed images of Flynn as a newborn, eating her first solid food, her first steps, covered in birthday cake on her first birthday, and many more snapshots chronicling the three years of her life. The final picture was one she must've taken in the past few days: Flynn sitting on my arm, both her hands are on my cheeks, and our foreheads touching. I had to leave the room for a minute.

Later, my sister and Tana took Flynn outside to try her new toboggan, and Betty and I started on dinner while Maxim took a nap on the couch.

-

Maxim squints as he stares me down.

"We won't hear of it," his wife throws her own objection on the table.

I try making my case with her, since he doesn't look in the mood to listen. "Your husband is recovering, and with the store closed, I'm sure you'd like some time among yourselves. It's not a big deal, only for a few nights before we start heading home."

"All the more reason to stay where you are. We have the room here, it doesn't make sense for you to check in to a hotel for just a few nights. You'll stay." She picks up her knife and fork and starts eating. Dismissed.

"You heard my wife," Maxim confirms when I look to him, and just like her, concentrates on his food.

Tana's soft chuckle has me turn to her. She's clearly amused at the exchange. "Guess I'm not the only one who wants you to stay."

"I'd like to stay," Leena adds in a soft voice, sending me a pleading look. Maxim snorts at that, and Tana's mom lets out a giggle.

Not wanting to be left out, Flynn weighs in too, although I doubt she understands what's going on.

"Stay!" she chirps, banging her spoon on the table with great enthusiasm.

"Bossy lot, aren't you?" I mutter, before shoving my fork in my mouth. I know when I'm outvoted.

The entire table dissolves in laughter as my noble plan is unanimously vetoed.

Tana

"Are you sure you don't want to wait until Flynn wakes up?"

It's still dark out and freezing cold.

I've already said a teary 'see you soon' to Leena, who is sitting bundled up in the front seat, waiting for Matt and me to say our goodbyes.

Mom and Dad insisted on getting up early to send them off as well. I almost lost it when Dad pulled

Matt into a one-armed man-brace and thanked him—calling him, "Son."

These past few days went too fast, and I desperately want to hold onto him a little longer."

He cups my face in his cold hands and rubs his nose along mine.

"It's easier like this. She doesn't have to see me leave. If she's still up tonight when I call you, maybe we can FaceTime."

FaceTime—that's all we'll have for the next however long, until things are sorted here. Matt assured me that if it took more than a few months, he'd try to fly out for a couple of days to see us. One way or another, I'll have to be back before April, and the start of the outdoor markets.

"I love you. I'm gonna miss you so much…"

"Me too, Sweetheart. Me too." He slants his mouth over mine for a heart-wrenching kiss we pour everything we can't find the words for, into. "Inside, love," he orders. "It's too cold out here. I'm going to call you tonight."

I do as he says, realizing I'm making it hard for him to leave. Mom is waiting just inside the door with a warm embrace, and we end up watching his taillights disappear down the road from the front window.

"Best way to get through anything is to keep moving forward," Mom says softly from behind me.

CHAPTER SEVENTEEN

Tana

It's been a long eight weeks, with only Matt's daily phone calls to keep me going, but the end is in sight.

Dad is recovering nicely, although he's still adjusting to being home full time. Having Flynn to look after during the day while I've kept the bakery going helped, as did the fly tying kit Matt gave him for Christmas. After some initial failures, he seems to have mastered the skill, and in the past week or two has produced enough flies to last him the fishing trip to Montana he and Mom are planning for the fall.

There's been a lot of that—planning. As well as some serious heart-to-hearts about an attainable future for everyone.

There have been arguments too. Mostly between Mom and Dad, although I weighed in on occasion as well. It became clear quite quickly, once we put the word out there, that while there was plenty of interest to buy, finding someone who'd be willing to take on the responsibility of running the bakery with no vested interest would be difficult.

For Dad, the business had always been much more than just a means to an income. He saw it as his legacy, one he inherited and one he wanted to pass on. Except there was no one to pass it on to. That hit home with him when the deal for Best Bites to distribute product to two hundred and thirteen chain stores nationwide was signed, sealed, and delivered.

But I think the real breakthrough came when Mom sagely pointed out that his legacy was not defined by a brick and mortar business, but by the future his daughter and granddaughter were building.

The next day we were vetting buyers, and today I'm introducing the new owner to the staff she plans to keep on. It's not easy to walk away from something that's been a part of your life for as long as you can recall, but sometimes it's necessary to create opportunities.

The guys are busy piping eclairs onto baking sheets, but look up when we walk in.

"Pete? Paul?" I draw their attention to the woman standing next to me. "I'd like you to meet Ms. Forsythe, the new owner."

The woman steps forward and holds out her hand to Pete.

"Call me Mary…please."

Behind us, Dad chuckles. He's been looking forward to this moment since discovering his successor's full name.

-

"Don't you think you're taking this a little too far?"

Mom is facing off with my father in the kitchen when I walk in a few days later, her fists on her hips, a sure sign she means business.

Apparently Dad, feeling the weight of responsibility lifted from his shoulders with the sale of the bakery, is looking to take his show on the road. A stack of flyers boasting the latest state-of-the-art recreational vehicles litters the counter. Flynn is sitting in her high chair, munching on Cheerios, as her eyes flit from one to the other, oblivious to my entrance.

"What's going on?" I demand, walking over to my daughter to drop a kiss on her head before I stare my parents down.

"Your father has lost his marbles. He wants to sell the house, buy an RV, and drag me all over the continent. The man's already made an appointment with the realtor!"

"I told you we'd stop at Graceland," he grumbles. "Isn't that what you've always wanted?"

"That's not the point!"

Flynn and I are planning to head home in a couple of days, and the thought of leaving my parents to their now frequent bickering, without me as their referee, gives me a headache.

"Mom," I try in a calm voice. "Explain to Dad what the point is." I don't need to hear the answer, I can venture a safe guess, but it's important for Dad to hear.

"I've been married to this man for close to fifty years," she retorts, but the tears in her eyes take the sting out of her sharp tone. "I shouldn't have to explain that for most of those fifty years I've stood by his side while he lived out his dream. Working side by side with him to build that bakery into what it is today. Now that it's gone, I'd like to have a say, for once, in what the future holds. I'd like to have a chance for a dream of my own."

The tears are now running down her cheeks and my father looks at her as if he sees water burning. Totally clueless.

"I thought you loved the bakery," he mutters, clearly confused.

"I did, you big oaf," she sobs, snatching a length of paper towel off the roll to mop her face. "I loved it because it's what you wanted."

Dad clears his throat, not quite sure what to do with himself, and when he looks to me for help, I mouth, "*Ask her.*"

"Well, what is it that you want then?"

I roll my eyes at his gruff tone, but at least he's asking. Beggars can't be choosers.

"I want to be closer to my babies."

Two hours later, we have the beginnings of a plan.

Matt

"I need you to go out to Micucci's to pick up today's produce."

I just walked in the door when Gunnar corners me.

"Why can't they deliver?"

"Because the truck with our order was involved in an accident. They just called. Someone will have to go handpick what we need. They won't be able to get it out before tomorrow, and we need the stuff for the dinner crowd. Take my truck—it's bigger—but leave your keys, just in case" He shoves a list and his keys in my hand.

"Can't someone else go?"

Gunnar visibly grinds his teeth.

I'm sure he's had enough of my miserable moods, which set in about two days after I got back from Minnesota, and have been steadfast since then. He's not the only one, the rest of my Skipper family keeps a safe distance these days as well. Fuck, I can barely stand myself.

Except Leena. She doesn't even seem to notice my mood—she's too happy with her newfound freedom. I use the term loosely, since she's never far from a watchful eye for now. It was Syd's suggestion to offer her the empty apartment over the pub. She's learning to live on her own, building her confidence, but never has to look far for a friendly face or a helping hand. On top of that, she doesn't have to worry about how she'll get to work. She's helping Dino in the kitchen for now, until she starts college in September.

The only things even remotely able to put a smile on my face are observing how my sister slowly awakens to the big world around her, and my daily talks with Tana, and occasionally Flynn, when she's still awake.

God, I miss them something fierce. Even knowing it won't be long before they head back from Minnesota isn't enough to brighten my mood. At this point, every day is one day too long.

"I asked *you*," Gunnar finally says pointedly, and I immediately feel guilty. The rest of the crew has been at it since ten or eleven this morning. They're busy doing lunch. Besides, I've known the guy for eighteen years: I know he doesn't ask unless he has no other choice. I'm behaving like a bear with a burr up his butt.

I fish my keys from my pocket and hand them over. "Sorry. I'm just—"

With a sharp wave of his hand, Gunnar brushes it off. "I get it, but you've got to get your ass in gear."

Truth is, he does get it. I spent many a time in the past weeks in his company, over a beer at the bar or a scotch in his office, waxing poetic about Tana and Flynn. He knows what they mean to me.

I'd expected ribbing over the whole insta-love thing, but every one of my friends has found their own 'significant other' in the past few years. They don't question the validity or depth of my feelings.

Micucci's is a busy place any day of the week and it takes me forty-five minutes to scour the massive store to gather all the items on my list. By the time I get back to The Skipper, it's already coming on four.

The kitchen is empty when I carry in the boxes of produce. It's possible Dino, our chef, is having a beer at the bar out front. He doesn't talk much, but he likes to chat with one of our regulars, Arnie, from time to time.

I stack the vegetables in the appropriate bins in the large walk-in pantry, and cut up the boxes before tossing them out back, next to the bin. My phone rings just as I walk back inside.

"Hey, sweetheart," I answer when I see Tana's name pop up on the screen.

"Hi. How's your day?"

"Already too long. I'm not good at this waiting," I grumble, making her chuckle.

"I hear you."

"So how come you're calling in the middle of the day?"

"I have a favor to ask. I've been trying for the past two hours to get Flynn down. You know how she gets when she's too wired up." I hum sympathetically. "Anyway, I was hoping you could sing to her? I've tried but I can't carry a tune to save my life. Apparently my daughter has sensitive ears because she keeps telling me to hush. Could you? Please?"

I'd do fucking anything for her or Flynn, but I'd rather not be caught singing Christmas carols in February. Now that I would never be able to live down. "I don't know…"

"Man!"

"Hey, baby," I coo hearing Flynn's voice. Tana put me on speaker: she's putting the thumbscrews on.

"Wooweee, pweeze."

"Not fair, Montana," I feebly protest, even though we both know who wins.

Still, as I start singing the first lines of Flynn's favorite, the "Coventry Carol," I go in search of a place I won't be disturbed. Gunnar's office is a good choice since he's generally home when his kids come out of school, for at least a few hours. I push open the door and I hear the words from my mouth reverberating back to me.

I freeze in the doorway when I see Tana, carrying her daughter, coming toward me.

"What?"

"Surprise," she says, smiling as she pulls my head down for a kiss, which is all the encouragement I need. Folding both of them in my arms, I cover Tana's mouth with mine, showing her exactly how much I've missed her. It takes me a while to notice a squirming Flynn wedged between us, who is trying to get my attention, or the applause and catcalls from the traitorous bunch of so-called colleagues.

It takes Gunnar's booming voice to herd everyone out, so we can have a moment in private. I have a ton of fucking questions, but I not so patiently wait for the crew to file out first.

"Good to see you smile," Syd says with a mischievous grin, and I'm sure she's had something to do with this.

"About bloody time." Viv, the pub's manager, and my longtime friend punches my shoulder in passing. "Although for the life of me, I can't imagine what she sees in you," she teases with a wink.

The big chef is next, and I know it's coming. "Who knew you had such a lovely singing voice."

Tana hides her face in my shirt, but I can feel her chuckle. I'll deal with her later.

"Bite me, Dino," I mutter under my breath as he passes, but little pots have big ears.

"Bite me!" Flynn chirps, and I roll my eyes to the ceiling when she giggles at the sound of her own voice. It'll be a while before she gets tired of that one.

Gunnar is last and claps me on my shoulder, grinning. "Good luck with that. You have the weekend off. Go home." He hands me my keys and I give his back. "The bags are in the back and a child seat is installed." He leans into Tana and gives her a peck on the cheek. "Good to finally meet you. It'll do wonders for his mood, I'm sure."

I wait firing off my many questions until I have Flynn safely strapped into her seat, and we're pulling out of the driveway.

"How did you get here so fast?" I ask, grabbing for her hand and entwining our fingers.

"We flew."

"But—"

"We had a meeting of the minds the day before yesterday. I can give you all the details later, but the short version is I couldn't wait to see you, and this was the fastest way to get here. Dad got it in his mind that he wants to drive across the country, so he and Mom will drive my car and hopefully, eventually, get here in one piece. And Mom is happy as a clam since she doesn't have to wait long to see us again. She'd like to be closer to us."

"As in move here?"

"Maybe," Tana says, smiling at me. "They're working out the details, but it may involve them taking over my place in Haverhill."

"No shit." It comes flying out of my mouth before I can check it, and I throw a quick glance over my shoulder to find Flynn already nodding off.

"No shit," Tana confirms softly.

"So does that mean you're definitely moving up here?"

"Looks that way."

I can't help the stupid grin I know is plastered on my face as I turn into my street and pull in my driveway. Turning off the engine I turn to her.

"Any idea where?"

Her eyes flick to my modest two-bedroom house before she looks back at me.

"I was kinda hoping…here?"

It takes me two seconds to get out and around to the passenger side, where I yank open her door and pull her from the vehicle. Her arms circle my neck and her legs wrap around my hips.

"Then welcome home, Sweetheart."

THE END

ACKNOWLEDGMENTS

As always, I thank my editing team: Karen and Joanne, who work so hard to perfect my words and guide me every step of the way.

My beta readers on this book: Debbie, Pam, Sam, and Deb, who scrutinize my story, and give me such helpful feedback every time.

I can't forget the ever-growing group of readers in my Barks&Bites group, whose support is invaluable.

I'm grateful for the always wise counsel and valued friendship from my agent: Stephanie of SBR Media.

Thank you to Ena and Amanda of Enticing Journey, who help promote my new book releases, and do with great care and professionalism.

A very special thank you this time to my publicists, Debra and Drue of Buoni Amici Press. In the short five or so months since we started working together, they have helped my growth and visibility in a way I could never have accomplished on my own. These ladies know their business and I have no idea how I survived so long without them.

As always, the greatest thanks belongs to my readers. To all of you who decided to take a chance, and dove into one of my books for the first time. There are pieces of me in each and every one of my stories and I'm honored you spent your valuable time reading them. Love you all.

ABOUT THE AUTHOR

Freya Barker inspires with her stories about 'real' people, perhaps less than perfect, each struggling to find their own slice of happy, but just as deserving of romance, thrills and chills, and some hot, sizzling sex in their lives.

Recipient of the RomCon "Reader's Choice" Award for best first book, "Slim To None," Freya has hit the ground running. She loves nothing more than to meet and mingle with her readers, whether it be online or in person at one of the signings she attends.

Freya spins story after story with an endless supply of bruised and dented characters, vying for attention!

www.freyabarker.com

ALSO BY FREYA BARKER

CEDAR TREE SERIES:

SLIM TO NONE
HUNDRED TO ONE
AGAINST ME
CLEAN LINES
UPPER HAND
LIKE ARROWS
HEAD START

PORTLAND, ME, NOVELS:

FROM DUST
CRUEL WATER
THROUGH FIRE
STILL AIR

SNAPSHOT SERIES:

SHUTTER SPEED
FREEZE FRAME
IDEAL IMAGE
PICTURE PERFECT (coming soon!)

NORTHERN LIGHTS COLLECTION:

A CHANGE IN TIDE
A CHANGE OF VIEW
A CHANGE OF PACE

ROCK POINT SERIES:

KEEPING 6
CABIN 12
HWY 550 (coming soon!)

STANDALONES:

BURNING FOR AUTUMN
(Susan Stoker's Badge Of Honor World)
January 8, 2019

FROM DUST

Want to learn more about *The Skipper* and Matt's family of friends?
Read on for a sample of Syd and Gunnar's story in FROM DUST, book #1 in the Portland ME series.

Syd

It's cold.

I think it's April, but I can't be sure. I haven't been interested in staying connected to the world for so long now, I couldn't even tell you the day of the week, let alone the time of day. I generally take my cue from what I feel and see. When the sun starts going down, I know the wharf will be virtually abandoned, and I feel I can finally leave the small shed that has been my home for a while now … a few months? Maybe it's been a year already, I couldn't tell you with the way time just seems to drift on endlessly.

The seasons are usually pretty easy to distinguish, but we've just had a particularly cold winter and it feels like it is lingering too long. I feel like I've been wearing every last stitch of clothing in my possession for a very long time now. It's been a bitch trying to get them clean at the outdoor tap on the edge of the dock. There've been many times this winter that I've gone rank with the cold temperatures; too cold to peel off even one of the layers of clothing to wash them, or myself for that matter. Who cares anyway?

Tonight I have a particular destination in mind. I heard the big delivery truck rumble past my shack earlier today, heading for my *neighbor*: a pub and grub called The Skipper. That usually means it's Thursday, because on Thursdays, The Skipper serves an all-you-can-eat menu, and that means that tonight, the dumpster in the alley behind the pub will be rich with leftovers.

I usually wait until I'm sure the place is good and locked up, but I haven't eaten more than a few bites of an apple somebody had discarded on the dock the day before yesterday. It only had a few bruises and I washed it carefully at the tap, but those few, richly flavorful bites put a rare smile on my face. It's not often I manage to get my hands on anything *fresh* tasting, let alone a whole apple.

I guess I could panhandle and buy some food like I've seen a few others do, but something holds me back, no matter how hungry I get. Begging would not befit a Donner, or so my parents have hammered into me. Funny, that after all these years, *that* is still as deeply ingrained as guilt is for a good Catholic.

I shake my head before my thoughts start drifting into areas I don't want to visit and pull my flannel shirt tighter around my shoulders to ward off the chill. *Damn, it's cold.*

Keeping to the shadow side of the alley, I tentatively edge my way to the dumpster that promises food for a few days, keeping my eye out for the big motorcycle that is often parked right beside it. Its usual spot is empty, which means the big, burly, and angry looking man isn't here tonight, or he's left already. I watch him sometimes when he drives by. I've come to the conclusion he must work there since he's there quite often. With that dark and dangerous air about him, it's difficult to keep from looking when I hear his motorcycle rumble past my shed. But tonight the coast is clear, and it appears the place is shut down. The only visible light is the weak bulb above the pub's back door, and that is on all the time.

My stomach starts rumbling, already reacting to the food smells wafting from the dumpster. When it comes to food, I'm thankful for the lingering cold weather. There have been too many times in the heat of summer where I've been so overwhelmed with the stench of a garbage can or dumpster, that I wasn't able to stop from puking, but not so tonight. Tonight

I can smell frying grease and garlic. The odd hint of herbs and spices filters past my olfactory sense. I'm hungry and my mouth is watering.

Using the dumpster's frame, I climb up and over the side, trying to be as quiet as I can—just in case. When I settle my feet amid the garbage, I scan the immediate area around me. *Jackpot.* A box of now familiar looking paper packages sits within reach. One of the things I've come to appreciate about hopping The Skipper's dumpster is that they wrap the leftover food in the paper lining of the baskets it's served in. Then they gather them all in one of the delivery boxes until it's time to dump them out. As a result, the leftovers are relatively untouched and it somehow makes the food taste better. Weird how once the thought of eating anything someone else had touched—let alone discarded—would have been enough to make me gag, but now, I'm just grateful. Grateful for the prospect of a full belly, and with the chill still in the air, the option to save some for another day before it spoils.

"Please don't."

The soft plea freezes me with a french fry halfway to my mouth. So preoccupied with stuffing my empty stomach, I didn't hear anyone approach. My hand drops the fry and I scramble to the far corner of the dumpster, looking up from under my eyelashes at the woman peeking over the side of the dumpster. I've seen her before; a tall blonde, about my age, with blue streaks through her hair. I've seen her go in the back door of The Skipper before and guessed she was an employee.

Her soft eyes and half-smile fill me with shame. Pity is devastating when it's directed at you, and I've never felt it as strongly as I do now. Wrapping my arms around my waist against the chills running through my body, I turn my eyes away so I can avoid looking at myself through her eyes.

"I'll make you something fresh. Do you want to come in out of the cold?"

My eyes flick to the back door before returning her steady gaze and I shake my head. The thought of being exposed to more pitying eyes would surely undo me. As tempting as it would be to walk through that door behind her and be able to sit down to a plate of food, I'm scared that I won't be able to return to this bleak existence I've resigned myself to afterward.

"I'm the only one here. We've closed up for the night and I was just putting the last of the garbage out." She winces at her own words, probably realizing the implication of her garbage reference. "Please …"

When she reaches her hand out to me, I can't resist stretching my own to touch it. It's been so very long since I've had any direct human contact that the moment our fingers touch, tears I thought had dried up long ago start rolling down my face. A craving to bask in her warmth some more has me following her gentle pull on my hand and I find myself clambering over the side of the dumpster. Meekly, I follow behind as she leads the way through the back door without a word, only stopping briefly at the threshold. The warmth rolling out of the open door is so inviting, I hesitate, wondering if I step through this door—if I allow myself this comfort—will I ever be able to turn back again. My heart pounds in my chest as I force myself to follow the woman inside the dark hallway, letting the door fall shut behind me.

Gunnar

I hear Viv yelling at me, but can't take my eyes off that scrawny pile of bones with the biggest eyes and gorgeous copper-colored mane of hair, sitting on my washroom floor.

I need to piss like you wouldn't believe and I'm this close to fucking wetting my pants like a child. Tearing my eyes away from whoever she is, I stalk past her and relieve myself in the first stall, not bothering to close the door. No time. A groan escapes me when I can finally let go. Fuck, that feels good, and I don't give a damn that I'm standing here pissing with an audience behind me. I've been on the road for a long fucking time and haven't been able to hit a washroom since the plane I was taking back to Boston from Phoenix hit a pocket of turbulence halfway through the flight. That nasty-ass stewardess—or flight attendant it is these days—was blocking the damn door and sent me back to my seat. Probably because I didn't care for her obvious come-ons. But who the fuck makes suggestive remarks to a guy who is obviously traveling with two kids? *A skank.* The moment we landed, we got stuck in a flow of people and I don't particularly like leaving the kids unsupervised outside an airport bathroom. I figured I could hold out until we were on the road but decided to just hoof it to the bar, first dropping off my guys at their mom's. Of course she picked that moment to start bitching about dumping the kids on her when we had already agreed on this schedule change weeks ago via e-mail. I've been gone for a week with them, visiting my mom, and told Cindy I'd drop them off around 3 p.m. because I'd need to check on the pub. I trust Viv, but it's a lot to take on my shift as well, and for an entire week at that.

"Jesus, Gunnar. Close the door, will you? You're gonna have Syd here quit on her first day!" Viv yells as she slams the stall door closed. Some mumbling and shuffling of feet follow and I'm glad to hear the washroom door slam shut as well.

Syd? That little thing's name is Syd? What kind of fucking name is that for a girl? My stream downgrades to a trickle. I shake off and tuck my business away, zipping up as I push open the door to get my hands washed. The washroom is empty. Seems Viv has taken her new charge out of here and is probably somewhere, trying to calm the little bird down. Christ, she looked like she was terrified. I feel kind of bad about that but holy shit, my bladder was bursting and I find some weird chick on the floor of the men's room.

I splash some water on my face in an attempt to rinse away some of the travel fatigue etched on my face. I'm getting fucking old at forty-four.

There are voices coming from the kitchen so I stick my head in to find the little bird sitting on a chair and Viv fussing over her. I better get this apology shit over with since I know Viv well enough to know she'll make my life hell if I don't. One reason why she handles all hires and fires is because I apparently don't have *people skills..* My people skills work well enough when I pour drinks. Plenty of women appreciate my people skills too. At least, I think they do, although it's not in my nature to check up with them after I leave them well-fucked in their beds. Never mind. Don't bring that shit home … not ever. My kids are with me every other week and that house is as much theirs as mine. My eyes turn back to take in that fantastic hair falling over the creeped-out chick's back. She has streaks of blonde in different shades, but the overall effect is of burnished copper.

Amazing for someone looking so gaunt everywhere else to have such bright bluish pools for eyes and a mass of shiny hair.

Sucking in a deep breath, I move into the kitchen. Viv lifts her head when she sees me approach and throws me a cautionary glance. The little bird, or Syd—whatever her name is—picks up on it and slowly turns around. The moment she looks me straight in the eyes, I have to suck in another deep breath. She must've been a knock out once, but the dark circles around those expressive eyes, the prominent cheekbones, and sharp chin are evidence of a hard life. Damn. What has Viv dragged in now?

"*Ahem.* So … I guess I should apologize for barking at ya," I tell her, noticing the long waves framing her face. She flicks her eyes down and seems to disappear into herself without saying a word. "I've just been on the road—long trip. I didn't expect to find a woman crawling around in the men's room. Sorry if I scared you."

It's becoming increasingly uncomfortable talking to this little person sitting frozen in front of me, refusing to meet my eyes again. I glance at Viv, who gives me a little smile of encouragement. *Jesus.*

"So, yeah … Syd, is it? Welcome to The Skipper. I'm Gunnar, but I guess you probably heard Viv call me that already. Anyway," slowly her head comes up as she focuses her eyes on me again, "glad to have you on board." I stick out my hand and she tentatively slips her tiny one in mine. A little squeeze and she pulls right back, but not before I feel the hair on my arms stand up from the charge that comes from touching her.

"Thanks."

Her voice is like rough sandpaper—so unexpected from a petite frame like hers.

"Right. Gonna check on the pub. Meet me in my office in half an hour?" The last I direct at Viv, whose smile has morphed into a smirk. *Smartass*. She can probably tell I can't wait to get out of here. With one last nod at Syd, I turn on my heels and make myself scarce.

For more on Syd and Gunnar, and the rest
of the crew at The Skipper:

FROM DUST

9 781988 733333